Florida Keys Short Stories

Fictional Island Stories Sprinkled with History and Reality

ABSOLUTELY AMAZING BOOKS

Habent Sua Fata Libelli

ABSOLUTELY AMAZING BOOKS

Manhanset House
POB 342
Shelter Island Hts., NY 11965

bricktower@aol.com • www.AbsolutelyAmazingebooks.com

Library of Congress Cataloging-in-Publication Data
Kadar, Wayne Louis "Skip."
Florida Keys Short Stories
p. cm.

1. FICTION / Short Stories (single author).
2. FICTION / Southern.
3. FICTION / Small Town & Rural

Fiction, I. Title.

ISBN: 978-1-955036-95-5, Trade Paper

Copyright © 2025 by Wayne "Skip" Kadar

October 2025

Florida Keys
Short Stories

Fictional Island Stories Sprinkled
with History and Reality

Skip Kadar

CONTENTS

Introduction 1

Tourist Season 3

Hurricane Irma 6

A Key West History Lesson 10

The Cell Phone 17

Jacques Cousteau Would be Proud of Me 25

The Cigar Box 31

The Last Will and Testament 34

A Statement of Unrequited Love 46

Online Dating 56

Nature Called 65

The Yellow Jeep Wrangler 70

Out of Character 74

The Buoyant Bra 81

A Wizard of Oz Moment 84

An Attack of Nature 87

Road Rage 91

It's an Invasion 96

Things that go Bump in the Night 104

Frank Sinatra Is Missing! 111

The Conch Republic Revolution 114

The Missile Silo 118

The Muddy River Tavern Duval Street Bar Crawl 123

The Helicopter Ride 129

Big Pine Key, More than Little Deer 134

A Nasty Sona Bitch 139

A Blessing or a Curse 146

About the Author 152

INTRODUCTION

The Florida Keys are a paradise rich in history, folk lore, mystery, colorful characters, natural geological creations and tropical splendor.

Nature shaped the islands; a million years of coral growth created the islands in the warm shallow waters of the Straits of Florida. Over time countless hurricanes and tropical storms assaulted the archipelago, bringing fresh water and new growth. Man, also shaped the islands by filling in between the Keys for a railroad bed and later a highway and greedy developers dug and blasted hundreds of miles of canals to create expensive waterfront property.

The diversity of the people who inhabited the Florida Keys are responsible for shaping the culture of the area. The inhabitants of the islands are a conglomeration of the indigenous Calusa Indians, Spanish explorers, the Bahamians who traveled to the fertile waters of the keys to fish, Cuban refugees seeking freedom, post-World War I and II veterans looking to make a new life, artists and writers who took inspiration from the islands and the invasion of masses of tourists seeking a warm winter. Inhabitants in the past were also drawn to the Florida Keys for sponging, turtle harvesting, cigar making, wrecking, treasure hunting and an occupation, which was very profitable, the importation of illegal drugs.

The short stories contained here are a glimpse into the history of the Florida Keys, its points of interest, its natural beauty, places where man touched the tropical paradise for the good and not so good reasons. The collection of short stories is fiction interspersed with fact of the sunny islands full of shady characters.

TOURIST SEASON

She knew she probably shouldn't have left her motel room alone. A guest at the breakfast buffet said he heard there was some nut up in Key Largo, or was it Islamorada, who posted online he was going to start hunting tourists, just like they hunt deer up north. He called it Tourist Season.

She didn't wake her roommate for this late night, or early morning walk, because Susan really, really enjoyed Duval Street and was passed out, fully dressed, diagonally across her bed.

She and Susan were lifelong friends since meeting in Mrs. Kadar's 1st grade class. They picked each other up when they were down, they were each other's shoulder to cry on, they celebrated each other's successes, they were together through high school, college, weddings, childbirth, Susan's two divorces, and now Susan was her emotional support as her marriage was on the brink of divorce.

She read online about the crazy person in Key Largo, she figured he was in the Upper Keys, and in his online manifesto he was going to kill the tourists ruining the pristine beauty of the Florida Keys and the developers raping the islands by building condominiums and resorts. She was in Key West, 95 miles away, and she wasn't doing anything to destroy the beauty of the Keys. She wasn't staying in a condo or a big resort, she and Susan were at the cute, meticulously landscaped, Pink Hibiscus Bed and Breakfast off Truman Avenue and yesterday she even filled a bag of litter she picked up from the beach. She was conscious of her life on this planet and did her part to preserve and protect it.

Strolling along the beach on the warm night she found mentally therapeutic, soul soothing. She slid off her sandals to feel the sand scrunch between her toes and loved the squeaking sound each step made at the water's edge. She hoped it would help with her mood. "What did they call it in old movies? Melancholy. That's it, I'm melancholy. It sounds better than being depressed."

It was dark. Hours ago, the warm subtropical sun had dipped below the horizon chasing the tourists from the Key West beaches to the Duval Street bars.

She had a decision to make. It was stressing her. She hoped the sound of the waves breaking on the shore and the gulls screeching on the wing would help with the dilemma. She paused to look out at the ocean. A cruise ship was on the horizon, its lights reflecting off the water of the flat calm Atlantic Ocean. There were a billion stars in the moonless sky.

There wasn't anyone around other than the couple she saw as she walked the beach. They were covered with a beach towel. She knew what they were doing. She had done it on a beach under a towel too. Not a Florida beach, it was the shore of Lake Huron, with a guy she thought she would spend the rest of her life with, a high school boyfriend. That didn't last, it was long ago, a few men ago, past loves from her 62 years.

She sat down, taking the small purse she bought from a Duval street vendor from around her neck, thinking of past loves, past mistakes. She picked up a handful of sand and let it sift through her fingers, staring out into the ocean. The sky lit up with the glow of distant lightning. She wondered if it would stay offshore or if it would be another storm for her to weather?

"It's like my life," she thought. "Periods of tranquility interspersed with thunder and lightning, pleasure and pain, laughter and tears, success and failure, ecstasy and agony."

On the beach, listening to the waves, feeling the warm southern breeze on her face, watching the stars in the sky, helped to calm her, helped to clear her mind. She smiled. The decision came to her as if it was made by a spirit from on high. The dilemma that had so tortured her was resolved, a sense of relief flooded over her, the veil of despair dissolved. She would forgive her husband. They had been together for too long, been through too much to toss it all aside. He made a mistake, she had made mistakes through the marriage too. But she didn't get caught.

With the decision made, the weight off her shoulders, she thought, "I'd better get back to the B&B. But first I have to get up. What did my mother always say as she got older; "Don't get down without a plan on how to get up." No one was watching, she didn't need to be graceful. She leaned her old yet still somewhat agile body forward onto hands and knees and grunted un-ladylike as she pushed herself vertical. "Who said these are the golden years? My joints feel more like it's the rust years."

She stood, brushing sand from her shorts, taking one last look at the ocean, at the ship; its portside lights red against the dark of night. Being there, her decision made, she felt peace in her life. She smiled, looked at the distant sky sporadically lit with lightning when a bullet pierced the back of her skull. Bone, blood and brain strewn to the sand.

It was the opening day of Tourist Season.

HURRICANE IRMA

Eric Miller sat in his brother's living room in Newnan, Georgia switching between the Weather Channel and CNN. Since evacuating his home in Islamorada, he had been glued to the TV, obsessed with watching as hurricane Irma made its slow approach towards the Florida Keys.

He was worried about his house, worried the roof couldn't withstand Category 4 or 5 winds. He was worried about his boat. It was trailered and parked close to his house but if the winds got to it, his Boston Whaler would be reduced to shredded fiberglass. He was concerned about Santiago Dominguez, his eighty-three-year-old neighbor who refused to evacuate, and Eric worried what the hurricane's storm surge would do to Anne's Beach.

Located at mile marker 73.5 in the upper Keys, Anne's Beach is a rarity in the Florida Keys; it's a natural sandy beach. Most of the beaches found on the island chain were trucked in from sand pits on the mainland or sucked up from the ocean's bottom.

Developer's were intent on exploiting the beach's natural beauty by building a condominium complex. But local environmentalists, led by Anne Eaton fought the development.

Mrs. Eaton was a teacher by profession who was paralyzed at the age of 24 after contracting polio. She married a wealthy man from Ohio, and in the 1960's they moved permanently to the Keys. Mrs. Eaton became an activist against over development and helped raise the money to preserve the stretch of beach. In 1992 the Monroe County saved the sandy strip along U.S. 1, made it a county park and named it, Anne's Beach, after Anne Eaton.

Since his wife left him, Eric became an Anne's Beach volunteer, he spent three or four days a week walking the beach welcoming the beachgoers, picking up trash and collecting hermit crabs living in empty seashells. He enjoyed walking the Anne's Beach 1,300-foot-long boardwalk showing the hermit crabs to tourists sitting at one of the six pavilions enjoying a picnic lunch and the view of the Atlantic Ocean.

Eric missed his wife, but as he told his friends and relatives, she just didn't want to be married and after one of their many arguments she packed up and left. The police received a call from a lady in Coral Gables stating that she suspected something bad had happened to her sister. Being her husband, and the spouse is always suspect number one, the police interviewed Eric, but nothing came from the investigation.

The Weather Channel's Jim Cantore provided Eric minute by minute Hurricane Irma updates. The meteorologist reported that Irma developed from a tropical wave near the Cape Verde Islands on August 30, 2017. And conditions were right to allow Irma to rapidly intensify into a Category 3 hurricane. By September 4th the storm intensified to Category 5 and slammed into the Leeward Islands, Antigua and Barbuda were left barely inhabitable.

The monster storm smashed Puerto Rico, northern Haiti and dumped 15 inches of rain on the Dominican Republic and the storm's outer bands were felt as far away as the Turks, Caicos and Bahamas.

By September 9th Irma struck Cuba with 150 miles per hour winds and 36-foot waves. The Cuban landfall weakened the storm to a Category 3 storm.

Eric watched the Weather Channel meteorologists explain that the storm would again strengthen over the warm waters of the Straits of Florida, separating Cuba and the Florida Keys. The experts took into consideration the impact of geography and steering currents of high and low meteorological cells to try to predict where the storm would make landfall along the Florida Keys. At first, they said the Upper Keys were in the storms bullseye. A stretch from Key Largo down through

Islamorada. Eric knew if it followed that path his beloved Anne's Beach would be destroyed. He prayed the storm would alter course and leave Anne's Beach alone.

Eric was relieved when Dr. Rick Knabb, the Weather Channel Hurricane Expert and Bryan Norcross the network Senior Hurricane Specialist, announced the storm would veer south and make landfall near Cudjoe Key, 20 miles north of Key West. The storm slammed into the Keys with a 10-foot storm surge and 10 to 15 inches of rain and Category 4 winds. Even though the eye of the storm went south it's effects were felt the entire length of the islands. Irma pummeled the Keys then proceeded into the Gulf of Mexico reduced to a Category 1 storm heading towards Marco Island and later again making landfall in Georgia as a tropical storm.

The destruction the length of the Florida Keys was devastating. Hundreds of homes and businesses were destroyed, and thousands of others were damaged. Anything not securely tied down was blown away or the monstrous storm surge swept it out to sea. But Eric was relieved the worst of the hurricane missed Anne's Beach. He was sure there was damage but he hoped the 1,300-foot board walk with its six pavilions and picnic tables had withstood the assault, especially the third pavilion from the north.

Eric switched to CNN to watch their coverage of Hurricane Irma's impact on the islands. Reporter Bill Weir was sitting in a destroyed Snapper's Oceanfront Restaurant and Bar in Key Largo interviewing the restaurant's owner. Eric laughed as the owner twice used the word "Shit" on the live telecast. It wasn't long before the broadcast feed was sent back to the CNN studios in Atlanta.

Eric was anxious to get back home to check on his house, his neighbor and Anne's Beach but Florida authorities closed off all access to the Keys to allow excavation equipment an opportunity to clean US 1 of storm debris.

Days later he got a call from his neighbor Santiago Dominguez who had ridden out the storm in his bathtub. He told Eric that his roof held but his Boston Whaler was off the trailer. It was blown against Santiago's garage with a large crack the length of its hull.

"Any word how Anne's Beach made out?" Eric asked his neighbor.

"I ain't seen it, cause there's shit all over the road, I ain't left my house, but I heard there ain't much of it left. I heard the waves took out the beach, there ain't no sand nomore."

Eric asked, "How about the boardwalk and the pavilions?"

"Don't know," Santiago replied.

Slowly over the days following Irma's landfall, inhabitants of the Keys were allowed to return and check their homes and businesses. After checking on his house and Santiago, Eric drove to Anne's Beach. Mounds of trash; furniture, mattresses, stoves, refrigerators and other household belongings ruined by the storm surge lined the highway waiting to be hauled away.

The entrance to the beach was barricaded off denying access, Eric parked on the shoulder of the road and walked in. The south parking lot was a mess; the asphalt surface of the parking lot was cracked and in many places missing, there were uprooted palm trees, mounds of sea weed, residue from the mangroves, broken sections of the boardwalk and other debris made walking nearly impossible. Eric wanted to get to the third pavilion to check for damage, but when he stepped on a board and a nail penetrated the sole of his shoe and the soft flesh of his instep, Eric turned around and hobbled back to his car.

Without electricity for lighting or cooking, Eric relied on emergency services to provide him with cases of bottled of water and food. One afternoon Eric answered the knock at his door expecting to find a hot meal, but standing at his door was a Monroe County Sheriff's Deputy.

"Mr. Miller, I would like you to accompany me to the station for a few questions."

The deputy withdraws a set of handcuffs from his belt saying, "Please turn around."

"Why? What's this all about?"

"Sir, the storm uncovered a female body partially buried in the sand under one of the pavilions on Anne's Beach. The injuries indicate the person died a violent death. Mr. Miller, the victim is your wife."

A KEY WEST HISTORY LESSON

He hoped the 593 miles from his home outside Valdosta, Georgia to Key West, would be far enough to help him forget about her. It was going to be hard; they had been together for two and half years. As he drove down the ramp onto I 75, he looked west and could see her apartment building, a few miles south he'd see the building where she worked, where she worked with Paul.

He crossed the Georgia / Florida state line his right blinker indicating his intention to make a stop at the Florida Welcome Center, home of the famous free glass of Florida orange juice. The parking lot was full of semi-trucks and SUVs packed with tourists. The memory of the first time he and Candy made the trip to Key West crawled into his mind. They had only traveled 18 miles from home, but she insisted she had to stop and pee at the welcome center. They laughed as he playfully teased her that she only stopped for the free orange juice.

As he walked back to his car, he mumbled to himself, "I wonder why they quit serving orange juice? Just another disappointment in my disappointing life."

Most everything he saw or did reminded him of her. He couldn't even look at the passenger seat without remembering their last trip to the Keys; her bare feet up on the dash, hugging her pillow, lightly snoring, her hair disheveled as she napped, and he drove.

Now he drove in silence. It seemed like almost every song played on the radio reminded him of her. A road sign said Ocala was just head. Near Ocala he would leave I 75 and join the southbound parade on the Florida Turnpike. He remembered the argument he and Candy had as they drove through Ocala, he wanted to stop and tour the Don Garlits Museum of Drag Racing. She didn't want to. She prevailed; they drove past the museum.

He knew what was ahead, the billboards for the Ron Jon Surf Shop. Rather than take the time to tour the Don Garlits Museum they drove out of their way to Cocoa Beach so Candy could get a tank top imprinted with the surf shop's famous logo. "But I gotta say she looked hot as hell in that tank top. The tight-fitting top really showed off her breasts." He thought for a minute. "Now Paul is looking at her in that shirt, at her breasts."

He stopped at a Cracker Barrel and rented an audio book, hoping John Grisham's *The Reckoning,* would help him forget about Candy and pass the time as he drove the length of the Florida peninsula. It helped. At least until he stopped for the night outside Fort Lauderdale, then the nightmare of their breakup resurfaced.

After three cups of coffee, a do-it-yourself waffle, and a stale cheese Danish he got back on the road. His GPS said he was 188 miles from his destination. He hoped he had time to finish the audio book, he had to part ways with Mr. Grisham at the Cracker Barrel in Florida City.

The drive through the Keys was still a source of pain for him, everything reminded him of previous trips with Candy. Once they stopped the length of the Keys snapping photographs at the road side attractions; the steam boat, *African Queen* from the 1951 movie starring Humphrey Bogart and Katharine Hepburn, the Shell World gift shop between the divided highway, the Wild Bird Rehabilitation Center in Tavernier, the 40 foot lobster in front of the Rain Barrel, the board walk at Anne's Beach, they fed the tarpons at Robbie's, went to Marathon's Dolphin Research Center and Turtle Hospital, and climbed up Henry Flagler's old railroad bridge at Bahia Honda. He and Candy even drove off the beaten path to the No Name Pub on Big Pine Key, taking pictures of the tiny Key Deer on the way.

The memories were everywhere, he couldn't escape them.

When he arrived in Key West, he realized the trip was not going to help him forget about Candy. Her memory was around every corner; The Southernmost monument where they kissed while their photograph was taken, the Mel Fisher Museum where Candy put her hand into the enclosure to hold a gold bar, before someone stole it. The Shipwreck Museum where Candy flirted shamelessly with the narrator dressed as a pirate, and Mallory Square where they hugged and cheered with the rest of the people celebrating the setting of the sun.

After checking into the Inn on the Ocean at 2:00 o'clock, he laid on the bed, the sliding glass door open to the Atlantic, the waves breaking on the shore lulled him to sleep. It was a sound sleep, like naps are supposed to be. He dreamed of being on a boat sailing to the Bahamas. He was with a woman, but strangely it wasn't Candy.

He had slept most of the afternoon, the result of a sleepless night in a motel in Fort Lauderdale. He awoke refreshed, went for a walk grabbing a braut and Coke from a street vendor at Smathers Beach. As the sun set, he sat on the beach watching the lights of the shrimp boat fleet with their long outriggers stretching out from either side of the boat draped with nets and a squadron of seagulls following them. "They are out to catch their limit of Key West Pink Shrimp," he said to no one.

He watched the moon rise over the ocean and climb high in the sky. It was late and it was dark. But he felt the sensation of contentment. A calm that he had not felt since before Candy told him she didn't love him anymore. He was relaxed, Candy was no longer haunting his mind. Nothing mattered to him, he had no regrets, no fears, it was a surreal feeling. He sat on the beach, stared out at the ocean, involuntarily drawing circles in the sand. He realized he was at peace with his life.

Staring out over the water he felt a presence near him. He turned to the right and saw a woman. He didn't know how long she was standing there. He said, "Hi."

She said, "Hello."

"You know it wasn't always like this." She said looking out at the ocean. "This wasn't always here. It used to be a swamp."

"What wasn't always here? The beach?"

"Yes, they brought in barges of sand from the Bahamas to make the beach. Tourists like beaches. They made a beach where there wasn't one."

He rose and walked to the woman. "Hi, I'm Jacob."

She reached out with a delicate hand, took his saying, "I'm Amelia."

"You mean this was a swamp and to attract tourists they brought in a beach?"

"Yes, Key West is nothing like it used to be."

He said, "I'm a sort of a history buff. I've done research about old Key West and I find it fascinating. What else has changed?"

She said, "I love history too, it's my passion. Before there was a sunset celebration in Mallory Square ships docked there. Large wooden schooners bringing in bananas and other exotic fruit from South America and taking coconuts, pineapples and key limes north. There were smaller wrecking boats that raced to ships impaled on the reef to salvage the cargo and save the crew and large square riggers with rows of cannons. Duval Street was just a dirt road that ran from the Atlantic Ocean to the Gulf of Mexico. There were saloons but nothing like the door-to-door bars stretching the length of Duval Street now. And there were several bordellos to serve the desires of the sailors.

"There weren't any sunset celebrations with street performers pandering for spare change, back in the day people simply celebrated living through another day, to see another sunrise. Accidents and death were a way of life then. Some were wreckers killed, like John Housman who was crushed between his boat and the ship he went to rescue. Hurricanes killed many sailors at sea and citizens ashore. There was a polio outbreak and other diseases that plagued the island. At one time hundreds were employed rolling cigars and many died from the unknown relationship between tobacco and cancer. A lot of people died here in Key West; it wasn't the party town it is now. Just take a stroll through the cemetery."

Jacob found Amelia fascinating. She was pleasant, she was knowledgeable of local history, and she was beautiful. All the while they talked Jacob never once thought of Candy.

They sat on the beach for hours. She told him of old Key West. "In 1823 piracy was a problem and Congress ordered Commodore Porter to establish a naval depot in Key West to end piracy, turning Key West into a navy town."

An airplane flew overhead towards the Key West International Airport. She looked skyward saying, "Over where the airport is now were Mr. Whitehead's and Mr. Fitzpatrick's salt ponds. Saltwater was held in shallow ponds and slowly evaporated leaving the salt. Without refrigeration we needed salt to preserve food."

She told Jacob of the sponging industry. "Divers, mostly Bahamians, gathered sponges, processed them and sent them off to market. For a while Key West was the world's center for sponge harvesting. And there were so many turtles in the waters around the island they were hunted to the point of near extinction. Wreckers salvaged cargoes and crew from ships grounded on the reef making Key West the wealthiest city per capital in the United States for a period."

She told Jacob of the ship that ran aground on the reef with a cargo of pianos. "After salvaging the cargo there was a piano in just about every house on the island, but no one knew how to play. The mayor placed an advertisement in a New York City newspaper requesting piano teachers to move to the island."

Jacob found the woman intriguing, beautiful, charming yet mysterious. He wanted to know more about her. "Are you from Key West originally?"

"Yes, my father, Richard Kemp, sold furniture as a profession but he loved turtles. In fact, he discovered a previously unknown species of sea turtle, which was named after him; the Kemp's Ridley turtle."

"That's fascinating, is he still living in Key West?"

"No, unfortunately he passed away, he is buried in the Key West Cemetery on Laurel Street. I often visit his grave."

Amelia stood saying, "It's late, I must go."

"Wait," Jacob said jumping up, not wanting their time together to end. Meeting her and talking with her had changed him. Candy no longer was the driving force in his life. This woman, whom he just met, had somehow freed him of Candy. He had an overpowering desire to be with Amelia. He couldn't just let her walk out of his life.

"Can we meet again? Maybe have dinner tomorrow?

She smiled at him "I'm afraid I cannot dine with you. But possibly we'll meet again here at the shore."

Jacob went to the beach the next two nights in hopes of seeing Amelia, but all he found was a man passed out on the sand and some kids passing a joint around. He went to the Key West Cemetery and searched for Amelia's father's grave, maybe she would be there.

He remembered Amelia's father's name was Richard Kemp and he was buried somewhere along the cemetery street named Laurel. He walked in off Olivia Street, found Laurel Street and began reading each tombstone. One of the first he came across was that of, Minnie Elizabeth Otto. Engraved on her stone was the inspiring epitaph: "Her life was a beautiful morning."

On the corner of Laurel and Third Avenue Jacob found the final resting place of Richard Moore Kemp. The tombstone was pitted and worn with age; the inscription barely visible. He brushed away dirt from the stone and said aloud, "This man was born in 1825 and died 83 years later in 1908. He died over one hundred years ago. I would guess Amelia is between twenty-five and thirty, this can't possibly be her father, maybe this is the grave of Amelia's grandfather. I must have misunderstood her."

Jacob spent the day looking for Amelia's father's grave but found nothing on Laurel Street or any other street in the cemetery.

Quenching his thirst with a couple beers at the Green Parrot, Jacob asked the bartender if there was a historical society in Key West. He wanted to see if he could solve the apparent mix up with Amelia's father and grandfather.

The Key West Museum of Art & History is located in the 1891 Custom's House and Post Office on Front Street just steps from the Mel Fisher Treasure Museum. Jacob followed the directions he got from the woman at the welcome desk, climbed to the third floor and knocked on a door with a sign, Director of Conservation.

"It's open," came a response.

Jacob entered the room to find a middle-aged woman, wearing a blue cap embroidered with an white English D over short spiky bright red hair, pink shorts, a lime green top and white cotton gloves. She said, "Hi. Are you lost?'

Jacob replied, "Ah, I don't think so."

"Okay, I don't get many visitors up here. Come on in."

"I'm trying to find information about a Key West resident who has passed away."

"Did ya try the cemetery? That's where we keep the dead ones."

Jacob shook his head, "Yes, but it only created more questions."

The woman closed the book from antiquity she was reading, pulled off the gloves and reached a tattooed arm forward, "Lillie."

He took her hand and said, "Jacob."

"Okay Jacob, tell me about your dead guy."

"The other night I met a woman on Smathers Beach, and we talked about old Key West. She mentioned that her father was buried in the cemetery, but I couldn't find his grave, I found her grandfather but not her father."

"What is the man's name?"

"Richard Kemp." He answered.

"How was the woman dressed?"

"She had on a dress. A long one. A little bit unusual for the beach."

"Was she pretty?"

"Oh yeah."

"Was her name Amelia?"

"Yes, how did you know that? Do you know her?" Jacob asked excitedly, hoping Lillie knew where he might find Amelia.

Lillie sat down behind her desk and motioned Jacob to sit in the chair across from her.

"Jacob, the grave of Richard Kemp you found is the grave of Amelia's father. Amelia was born and raised here on the island but was attending finishing school in Philadelphia when her father died in 1908. She boarded a ship to Key West to bury her father, but the ship encountered a storm off the eastern tip of Cuba and sank. There were no survivors."

"No, that must be a different person. I was talking to her just two nights ago."

"No, I've been through this before with others who met the woman on the beach. The woman you met on the beach is Amelia Kemp, daughter of Richard Kemp. They both died in 1908, but she still walks the beach telling people of old Key West."

Jacob had an expression of bewilderment and disbelief on his face.

Lillie said, "Jacob, welcome to strange and mysterious Key West."

THE CELL PHONE

"Where's my phone? Shoot, where's my phone? Annika, did you take my phone? My phone is missing!"

"Don't go into panic mode. I'm sure it's here somewhere. When did you last use it?

Carrie dumping out her purse on the couch answered, "I don't know. I remember I got a call when I was at the beach."

"Is it in your car? Or maybe in with your beach stuff."

Returning from the driveway, Carrie nervously ran her fingers through her long blond hair, "It's not there."

"I'll call it and you listen for the ring. You probably set it down somewhere and just forgot where," Annika, Carrie's best friend, suggested.

Annika dialed, they listened, nothing.

"Go out to your car again and I'll call. Maybe it fell between the seat and the council like last time it was missing."

Carrie came in, "Nothing. Where is the damn thing?"

Annika had Carrie sit down and walked her through all of the places she had been since she last used her phone.

"I went to Sombrero Beach for a while, but it was packed with Spring Breakers. Why do they have to use our beach anyway?"

"Ah, because it's only the best beach in the Keys," Annika said. "Where did you go from there?"

"I stopped at the Walgreen liquor store, then Publix, then I went to Burdines to check when I work next and met Trevor for a beer, then came home."

"I remember I used it on the beach to text you but, I can't remember using it after that."

"Carrie, think. You're always on your phone, talking or texting. Think."

A white-haired woman turned on her blinker to take the parking spot recently vacated by a minivan, a red Camaro convertible coming the wrong way down the lane quickly turned into it. The older lady drove by and shook her fist at the young guy who took the spot just three away from the entrance to Publix. He laughed and gave the lady the finger. He looked down and noticed something sparkled on the ground. It was a cell phone in a rhinestone encrusted case lying on the asphalt. "My lucky day!" He picked it up, tossed it on the passenger seat and walked into the store to buy some bait and chum bags.

Sitting in his Boston Whaler with two more rods baited than was legal and nothing biting, he picked up the phone he found. He figured if he could turn it on he could find out who lost it and maybe snake a reward out of them. He looked it over, it was an Apple, no identifying markings.

He punched the button on the bottom of the phone. The screen gave the time and date then instead of asking for a thumbprint or a passcode it went right to the home screen. "No shit. It ain't password protected."

He checked out the apps on the phone. There were the usual, Messenger, Calendar, Camera, Photos, App Store, and a few the owner had downloaded; The Weather Channel, Yelp, Twitter, some fitness tracker, Cloze, Facebook, Instagram and a few more he never heard of.

He pushed the messenger tab. "Man this person must have never deleted a message, there are like a couple of thousand of em." The messenger app kept him entertained for an hour, he didn't even care if the fish didn't like his bait. From the phone he learned the owner was named Carrie. She was single and liked to party. She texted someone named Annika a lot, and was dating a guy named Trevor.

He pushed the Photos tab. "Wow, she must have three thousand pictures on here." He didn't know who Carrie was but he kinda narrowed it down to a blond who was in her late twenties and had a great body; a lot of bathing suit pics. She was in most of the photographs, posing with other girls and some guys so he figured it must be her. There was even a pic of the blond holding her arm over her bare boobs while a guy had his arm around her waist, there were other people in the background. "Man, I bet that was an awesome day."

The fishing sucked so he pulled lines and headed to shore.

He stopped at Publix and grabbed a six of Yuengling, a roasted chicken breast and an iPhone charger cord; he was an Android lost in an Apple world. Back to his trailer he plugged in the phone, opened a beer and before long there were chicken grease fingerprints all over the screen of the found phone.

He picked out Annika Fredrick from the contacts list and texted her.

"Carrie, I just got a text from you, someone found your phone. He asks me to tell the owner of the phone that they found it and wants to return it."

> Grabbing the phone, Carrie says, "Gimme that."
>
> Carrie on Annika's phone: "Yes, that's my phone. Where did you find it? I need my phone. Where can we meet."
>
> Carrie's Phone: "I found it in the Publix parking lot. If you want I can meet you somewhere. Is there a reward?"
>
> Carrie on Annika's phone: "I can do maybe twenty bucks."
>
> Carrie's Phone: "Twenty bucks doesn't do it. This phone is worth hundreds. It's gotta be more."
>
> Carrie on Annika's phone: "I don't have any more."
>
> Carrie's Phone: "Until you come up with more cash, no phone for you."
>
> Carrie on Annika's phone: "I'll see what I can do, I need my phone!"
>
> Carrie's Phone: "Then find some more reward money."

Marcy walked into Burdines and sought out Carrie behind the bar. "Hey, what's this shit you're texting me? I never hit on Trevor. I don't even like Trevor."

Carrie said, "Crap! Marcy, I lost my phone and whoever found it is texting on it.

"How did he know your password?"

Carrie looked down at the beer she was pouring, "I got tired typing in the password, so I deleted it."

"Your phone wasn't password protected? And now he has access to my phone? What's wrong with you? No one does that."

"I know, I'm sorry."

Back at Annika's apartment Carrie got a call on Annika's phone. "It's for you," Annika said to Carrie. A bit of disgust in her tone. "It's your mom."

"Honey, I got a call from your number and some guy was saying all kinds of terrible stuff. He said you had a venereal disease, and that you're pregnant, What's going on? Honey, are you okay? You know you can always talk to me."

Carrie explained the situation, how she lost her phone, how the guy who found it wants money, and he is calling and texting people on her call list.

"Hey Babe, what's up?" Trevor answered his phone seeing Carrie's caller ID.

A male vice said, *"Trevor, Carrie asked me to call you. She is done with you; she doesn't love you anymore. She wants you to leave her alone. She says she's not even sure if the baby is yours."*

Carrie stopped by the Sheriff's office to report that someone found her phone, was refusing to return it and was calling and texting her friends. They said they couldn't do anything; the guy technically hadn't done anything illegal.

Annika was next to receive a text from Carrie's phone.

Carrie's Phone: *"Hey, has Carrie come up with any more reward money?"*

Annika: *"Why are you such a prick? Just give her the phone back. Don't be such an asshole."*

Carrie's Phone: *"It's only fair that I get a reward for being a good Samaritan. I'm trying to do what's right. She's the one being cheap and holding out."*

Annika: *"Listen you son of a bitch. Give her back her phone. She offered all she can. Take the twenty bucks and go back into whatever hole you crawled out of."*

Carrie's Phone: *"Don't talk to me like that bitch! I'm trying to help out, be the good guy and return her phone and you're getting bitchy with me. Fuck you, you bitch!"*

Annika's phone began ringing, "Hello, oh hi Liz."

"Annika, I just got a text from Carrie saying she was in trouble and asking for money. Is she okay?"

Annika explained the situation of the lost phone and the jerk who found it.

Liz added, *"It was a group text, cause Linda, Bonnie, Sue, Karen, Debbie, Patty, Diane and Lynn, all got it too."*

Carrie and Annika told the deputy when he responded to their call, "I told you guys that someone had my phone but you didn't do anything about it and now look." She held Annika's phone out for him to see. "It's the guy who found my phone. He did this." The iPhone photograph showed Annika's two left tires were flat and "Fuck You Bitch" was scratched into the paint of her Camry.

"I'm just going to block Carrie's number so this will end," Annika said in desperation.

"No," the deputy said. "Don't do that. If he did this then he has committed a crime and we'll track him through your phone. We need to keep him calling and texting so we can use it to find him."

Carrie's Phone: *"Hey bitch, how's your car?"*

Annika called Deputy Radak when she received the text. "Try to keep him texting," he responded. She texted him but he didn't text her back.

Carrie's Phone: *"I know where you live and work, Bitch."*

Annika was both furious and scared. She called the deputy to report the threat.

"We tracked the calls and texts from your friend's number and found they pinged from all over the Keys; Key Largo, Marathon, Tavernier, Big Pine and Key West. The guy must be traveling the length of the Keys.

Carrie's Phone: *"I like your red bra and matching panties."*

When the deputy came to her door, Annika read him the texts.

"Are you wearing red underwear?" he asked.

She gave a look of disgust and pulled aside the neck of her tee shirt revealing a red shoulder strap.

"Sorry, I have to be thorough. Can I see your bathroom?"

Annika showed the deputy the room.

The lower half of the window was frosted and the upper covered with a curtain.

"Was the curtain closed?"

"Yes, of course."

"He couldn't have seen you through this window. Where is your bedroom?"

They walked from the bathroom to the adjacent room.

The deputy, pointing to the window said, "The curtain is drawn closed but not tight, the lower portion is open just a half of an inch. That would be enough for someone to peak in."

Outside the deputy found a couple of cement blocks had been placed under her bedroom window. "The guy stood on them to peak into your bedroom window."

Annika felt violated, she was shaking with the thought of a stranger watching her get dressed. "He probably saw me naked!"

"Do you have someone you can stay with for a while? You shouldn't be here." The deputy told Annika.

Annika told her friend, Mica, "No, they were not able to get any fingerprints from the blocks or the windowsill. But that son of a bitch was peeping at me dressing!", when she called to see if she could stay with him for a few days.

"Okay, you win you son of a bitch, I've got $200. Where can meet so I can get my phone back?" Carrie texted.

"I want $400." Came the response.

"I don't have $400!"

"So, find it. Ask Annika, ask your mommy, ask Trevor. I can make life much more miserable for you and your friends."

Deputy Radak said, "This guy has committed multiple crimes; extortion, window peeping, damaging personal property, we'll get you the money. Carrie, when he contacts you again tell him you have the money and want to meet. But make sure the meeting is somewhere public so you'll be safe and we can keep an eye on you and the perpetrator."

"Got the money?"

"Yes, when can I get my phone back?"

You know where Dillon's Pub is in up in Tavernier?"

"Yes."

"Tomorrow night around nine drive beyond the bar and turn right down behind the buildings. There is a dumpster behind Winn Dixie. To the right of it there will be an empty dill pickle jar lying on the pavement. In the jar there will be a note where to find your phone. Put the money in the jar. Come alone, I'll be watching."

With a sheriff's deputy in Winn Dixie secretly looking out the loading bay door and another further down the road watching, Carrie found the jar, took out the note and placed four one-hundred-dollar bills in the pickle jar. Movement by the dumpster startled her, a stray cat scurrying around the ground and another atop the dumpster. Carrie quickly ran from the dumpster to her car parked in front of Dillons. She locked the car doors and read the note.

"Go to the Holiday Inn in Key Largo. The phone will be in a bag behind a bush by the north side exit door."

Carrie backed out of her parking spot at Dillion's and pulled out on northbound US 1. An unmarked sheriff's car followed while other deputies remained to see who picked up the money. A deputy escorted Carrie from the Holiday Inn parking lot to the phone pick-up spot. At the bush, the deputy wearing latex gloves picked up the white plastic Publix bag. Carrie reached for it, he pulled away saying there might be fingerprints.

At the alley behind Winn Dixie, a man with a grey shaggy beard, long hair flowing from beneath his cap, dressed in a shabby coat too heavy for the warm evening, pushing a shopping cart filled with assorted belongings; a sleeping bag, a couple of plastic bags, a piece of blue plastic tarp, empty bottles and cans, a plastic jug of water, a half of roll of toilet paper and a bag of cat food came staggering along. The deputies watched him slowly walk as he talked to the cats parading behind him. He picked up a plastic mayonnaise jar that had fallen from the dumpster, opened it, and threw it towards the dumpster, missing it. The jar bounced, scaring a rat back into the mangroves. A pickle jar caught his attention next. He picked it up as the cats circled his legs waiting to be feed them. He looked in the jar, unscrewed the top and took out the four one-hundred-dollar bills. He quickly tucked the bills in his pocket. The man poured the bag of cat food on the ground and wheeled his cart out of the alley. The deputies followed at a distance. Wondering if this was him, the guy who was blackmailing Carrie or a homeless guy who just stumbled on a windfall of cash. The man crossed the parking lot towards McDonalds. Giving a driver the finger as he walked in front of a car heading to the drive thru lane, the man pushed his cart, stopping at a red Camaro convertible.

The deputies watched as the man pulled the bills he stashed in his pants pocket and handed them to the driver of the car. The driver handed something out the window to the man. A twenty-dollar bill and a plastic bag with a bottle of whiskey. The Deputies approached the car and detained both men.

"Carrie, it's over," Deputy Radak said as he handed the cell phone to her. We have arrested a man, and he has confessed to having your phone, sending fictitious texts, damaging Annika's car and looking in her windows."

The deputy continued, "He says it started as a joke, but escalated from there, he didn't mean to hurt anyone. He just got caught up in the game and saw an opportunity to make some money."

"Does he know the anguish and agony he put Annika and I through? She feared for her life after his threats, and he ruined my reputation. That is no joke. I hope the judge throws in a pit of pythons!"

"What's his name?" Carrie asked.

Checking his notebook again, Deputy Radak says, "Thomas Minor. Works for a liquor distributor. Travels the Keys, that's why the phone kept pinging on cell towers the length of the islands.

"He is in custody; you and Annika are safe now. I think he may have been sampling some of his own product."

"Good! I hope the judge hangs the son of a bitch!" Carrie said. "No, cut his balls off then hang him!"

JACQUES COUSTEAU WOULD BE PROUD OF ME

I've been at the big resorts with four star restaurants, three swimming pools a couple with swim up bars, and hundreds of guests but I really prefer these small intimate hotels. Here at the Island Beach Inn in the upper Keys it's cozy. On the small plot of land bordered by US 1 at the front, a small condo on one side, a private residence on the other and Florida Bay at the rear they have created a little slice of paradise. I have vacationed on the ocean side of the Keys but prefer the Gulf side, it isn't as windy as it is on the ocean, the water is calmer making for fantastic paddle boarding and kayaking. Not that I've done either.

This "Mini" resort has 12 rooms and bungalows, parking, and a beach all on this small postage stamp piece of waterfront property. It sounds crowded but the proprietors have done a nice job of landscaping to give it a comfortable rather than crowded feeling. Tall coconut palms block out a view of the condo next door, and you can't see the house next door due to the decorative wood fence and flowering foliage.

There isn't a pool with kids screaming "Marco... Polo" and guests reserving chairs with towels. There aren't servers carrying trays of colorful tropical drinks catering to your every whim, it's just relaxing. Just what I need peace and quiet to escape from the toils and troubles of my daily life.

Business has been good. It allows me time to sneak off on these sunny vacations and still meet parole and pay alimony to the bitch.

Laying on the lounger on the beach, I split my time between reading a compilation of short stories, *Murder in Key West*, watching power boats and kayaks pass by and looking at the young ladies down the beach. There are three of them, probably in their thirties, a pale skin redhead with globs of white sunscreen where it wasn't fully rubbed in, a blond wearing a pink bikini with a diamond bracelet on her left wrist, rings on most fingers of both hands and multiple piercing in her ears. She seemed to dominate the conversation and gestures wildly, her rings and bracelet glimmering in the sun. The third woman's hair was more of a chestnut color. She reclined in the sun reading a thick paperback book, ignoring her talkative friend. They all had drinks in stainless steel thermos cups with metal straws. I wonder what's in them? My imagination takes over, I bet "red" has a Mimosa. Chestnut probably has ice water and "Flashy" that's what I decided to call her, has a Margarita. When "Flashy" turned towards me I could hear what she was saying. Mostly she was complaining about a guy she is dating, saying that he is cute but doesn't live up to her standards, "Ya know fun to play with but nothing to take out in public."

She sounds like my ex-wife. Bitch, bitch, bitch. Never satisfied, always complaining. Criticizing me about everything. She was embarrassed that I parked my pickup truck in front of the house. Criticizing me about my weight. Now granted she has some standing there. When we were dating she called me chubby, and I was a little paunchy around the waist. I never was a dynamic specimen of the male physique. Even at my best I could still be used as a before photo in a health club advertisement. As proof of my physique, I'm lounging at the beach with the elastic on my tropical flowered swimsuit straining to hold back my stomach. On a vacation in Jamaica a few years back my wife said I looked like a blubbery seal laying on the beach. She would probably call me a beached whale now; I've put on a few pounds.

My wraparound sunglasses allow me to look forward but peripherally watch the three women. The chestnut has the best body of the three. Her boobs are not too big and not too small and nicely rounded and fantastic legs. "Red" is thin, bordering on skinny. Too thin for me I like a little meat on my women. The "Flashy" blonde is too blonde, too loud, too chunky, and too short for her weight. Her legs look like tree trunks and her much too small bikini is being swallowed by layers of excess flesh overflowing the fabric. Maybe she figures all the jewelry will distract from her otherwise large frame.

I'm sure I don't stand a chance with any of those women, so I turn my attention to enjoying myself here on the beach. I had always wanted to try snorkeling. It looks fun but I didn't want to do it on any of our Caribbean vacations where they take you out on a boat, miles from shore, give you a mask and tell you to be back to the boat in 45 minutes. That frightened me. I'm not a good swimmer, even with my body mass I don't float and there are creatures in the ocean who would look at me like I'm dinner for the whole family. I was reading something online about things to do in the Florida Keys and it said the Keys offer some of the best snorkeling in Florida. That's it, I'm going to face my fears and go snorkeling. Here I can walk in from the beach and the water isn't that deep, I can probably stand in most places.

I push my body up from the lounger, not very gracefully I admit, pull my suit out of my crack, and walk, trying not to waddle, to the box containing the resort's snorkeling gear.

I hear "Mouthy", yes I changed her name from "Flashy", say, "If that's the only single guy at this resort I'm going to shoot myself."

I return to my lounge chair with a mesh bag of all the gear I will need to explore the world below the waves. At least that's what the resort brochure said. I glance over at the girls and "red" is reapplying sunscreen, Chestnut is reading and "Mouthy" is gone. I notice someone swimming offshore and as her arm extended in a stroke I can see a diamond bracelet on her wrist. It's "Mouthy"

I adjust my yellow mask making sure it seals tightly, my mustache doesn't make it easy. I'm sure I'll be surfacing frequently ripping off a water filled mask. The one size fits all adult men's swim fins don't quite fit my chubby feet but with effort I pull them on and clumsily rise from the chair. I'm only 12 feet from the water's edge but the yellow fins made it awkward to walk. The first couple steps I tried walking forward I almost topple over head first in the sand, then I remembered what "Snorkeling for Dummies" said, walking backwards makes it easier, still clumsy but easier. I stepped backwards along the sand, getting yelled at by a little girl for trampling her sandcastle. I apologized profusely although through the snorkel sounding more like a male walrus grunting during mating season.

Two more steps put me ankle deep in the salty water of the Gulf of Mexico. I pause' to remove my mask. Trying not to look like a neophyte snorkeler I bend, almost falling forward, to swish my mask in the water, brought it to my face and spit in it. I'm not going to use the bottled "Spit" you can buy to coat my mask to prevent fogging, I'm using the natural method. My index finger smears the saliva inside the mask then I rinsed it in the water.

I survey the surface of the water, making sure the crocodile I heard was seen nearby wasn't lurking in the shallows. The lady at the front desk said it was just a rumor. I hope she is right cause my fat ass would tempt a croc for sure.

Fitting the mask back on my head, I don't have to worry about any head hair preventing a good seal, I don't have any. I exhaled blowing through the yellow snorkel just in case any spiders had climbed in while it was in the storage box. The thought of inhaling a spider would make me gag and run from the water screaming like a little girl. No bugs came out so I inhaled.

All systems seem ready to go. I slowly back in, my neck swiveling to the left and right to watch where I was going. One unseen chunk of coral could cause me to fall over. And I'd crush a child if I one is playing behind me. My breath is rapid and deep, trumpeting through the snorkel. When the water reaches the sensitive area of my swimsuit, I slow down so the relative coolness of the water doesn't shock the "boys."

With the water at my waist it's time to lean forward and assume the correct prone, face down snorkeling position. The spit didn't work, my mask is foggy, probably good since I can't see the people on the beach. I'm sure I'm entertaining them. I'm proud of myself for making it this far, conquering my fears, stepping out of my comfort zone, taking the plunge. Well about to take the plunge anyway. I suck in a big breath, hoping its not my last and fall forward.

I open my eyes, I don't know why I closed them I've got a mask on, and suddenly I'm in a whole different world. The sun penetrates the surface in shafts of shimmering light. Through the lens of the mask, the sandy bottom is dotted with specks of color, the seaweed is greener than it looked from above the surface and small fish dart around me. Hey, I'm floating! The saltwater supports my bulk unlike freshwater. And I'm breathing, just need to remember to keep the top of the snorkel out of the water or I'll suck in a mouthful. I relax looking about my surroundings. A few yards to my right I see yellow and blue striped fish, they ignore me but I'm fascinated with them. Below me a shell is moving leaving a trail, the legs of a hermit crab propelling it across the sand. A small barracuda is hovering in the water keeping an eye on me, I'm keeping an eye on him too, from a program on Discovery I know they have teeth. On that same program they said crocodiles live in salt water and alligators live in freshwater, or was it the other way around? There are probably not any of them around here, it's too busy, too many tourists flopping around in the water, jet skis buzzing around.

Snorkeling is amazing, it over stimulates you visually while there is very little sound, just my breathing. Just then a weird sound interrupts my tranquil existence. It's a winding noise. I stop moving, listening. It's getting louder, not real loud but louder. I raise my head out of the water my legs fall to the bottom. Looking around I see a powerboat zooming by quite a way away. It's amazing how sound travels in water. While out of the water I can hear a woman's voice from shore. I look back towards the beach and see "Chestnut" yelling and waving at me. Is she cheering me on? Is she impressed with how I overcame my fear. Hum, maybe "Chestnut" has taken an interest in me since I'm showing no fear and just enjoying nature. Maybe I have a shot with her? I wave back at her. I wonder if I should offer to take her to dinner. That Lorilei place I saw advertised looked nice. Or maybe that Brewery in Islamorada would be more to her liking. And I bought a new shirt at Shell World I can wear. I sink back in the water to show her I have no fear of the water, I'm a regular Jacques Cousteau.

I look around and the yellow and blue stripped fish are gone. The little fish that were darting around me are nowhere to be seen. The barracuda has turned and taken off, even the moving shell has stopped. My once tranquil world full of nature is now barren, just sand, seaweed, and the occasional chunk of coral. No sea creatures. Movement off to my right catches my attention. It's in the distance, I can't make it out, damn foggy mask and my insufficient spit. I kicked, propelling me towards it. "Shit!" I scream through my snorkel mouthpiece. "It's a crocodile! A big fucking crocodile!" I'm facing death and my mind thinks, "It's crocodiles that live in saltwater." It's not coming towards me, which is good because I'm paralyzed in fear, I can't move. It's swimming passed me about twenty feet away. It has something dangling from its mouth. It's an arm, a human arm with a diamond bracelet glimmering in the shafts of sun.

"I've got to tell someone; I've got to get help," he thought in his confused mind. Swimming as fast as he could, arms flailing and legs kicking wildly. He then lowered his legs to the bottom to run to shore. He took one step and fell.

He awoke, he was on the beach. It was just a dream; he had fallen asleep on the lounge chair. His head slowly cleared; he realized he was lying on the sand. In his attempt to get to shore for help in his dream, he had been kicking his legs violently and had fallen off his lounge chair.

The women down the beach were laughing hysterically.

THE CIGAR BOX

I bought this cigar box at a yard sale on Stock Island. I don't know why, it just appealed to me. The label on the cover of the box has faded over time but you can still read some of the lettering in Spanish. There's also an image of a well-dressed man sitting on a red upholstered chair, one hand holding a whiskey glass with ice cubes in the other hand a cigar between his index and middle fingers, the mustachioed man is blowing a plume of smoke into the air.

When I first bought the box, I could still smell the aroma of the cigars it once held. I wondered if the cigars came from the legendary tobacco fields of Cuba, now illegal in the United States. And my imagination had a Cuban craftsman working in a small shop carefully shaping the mahogany box, cutting precision joints at the corners, sanding it smooth, varnishing it to a deep rich glossy brown, assembling it with brass hinges and clasp.

For years the box sat next to my front door. When I came home, I threw my keys and loose change in it. Over time it also came to contain an expired wooden token good for a free drink at Captain Tony's, a nut that fell off my bike, a string of purple plastic beads from Fantasy Fest and a colorful seashell. The shell always reminded me of you. I remember picking it up on Smathers Beach when you and I were first together. You were so young then, running and frolicking on the sand. The tourists laughed as they watched you, unfamiliar with the ocean, wade out in the water then run back as a wave rolled in.

Now we're at the beach again. Just you and I, like it's been most of the time. You came into my life 11 years ago and we have been practically inseparable ever since. I admit that I wasn't looking for anyone to share my life with until I met you. I was in a bad way, Layla had left me, I was depressed, drinking too much. But when you entered my life, you gave me a reason to live. You saved me from despair, from the suicidal thoughts that rattled around in my head. The minute we met I knew I needed you in my life and I'm pretty sure you needed me. You gave me my life back.

You made me a better person. With you in my life I quit drinking, well, I quit drinking in bars and only drank a few beers at home with you. I hurried home, knowing you would be there waiting for me.

When I was crewing on the Happy Angler and came home stinking of fish you didn't complain. You were just happy I was home. Even when my manager said she didn't mind if you hung out while I was bar tending you sat there watching the people patiently waiting till I got off and we walked home.

There were times I was angry, mad at a boss or some entitled tourist, upset with my job, pissed my tips were low, but you always had a way to calm me down. I'd grab a beer from the fridge plop down on the couch, you cuddled up next to me and my troubles became just thoughts of the past.

When I owned our boat and went fishing you were always my first mate. We sometimes walked down Duval Street just watching the tourists. I was always so proud to walk with you. You turned heads. Guys and girls would take a second look at you. As we walked next to one another, I would occasionally catch you turn your head to look at me with adoring eyes. I had the same love and affection for you.

There were times we just needed to get out of Key West, get off the rock for a bit and we'd take a ride up US 1, stopping at Sombrero Beach in Marathon or Settlers Park in Tavernier. The highlight of our trip was always stopping at the Dairy Queen. We would get a couple of ice cream cones, mine chocolate yours vanilla.

It's evening, there aren't any tourists on the beach, they're all parading on Duval Street, shopping, drinking, eating and dancing at the bars. I'm standing knee deep in the ocean, waves splashing on my legs. We are alone, just the two of us. Tears trickle down my face as I open the mahogany cigar box and slowly drop your ashes into the ocean. I quietly thank God for sending you to me.

Stormy, you were the best dog ever.

THE LAST WILL AND TESTAMENT

This story originally appeared in Murder in Key West 7,
edited by Shirrel Rhoades

"Bud Light?" Ski asked.

The man, Rick Nash, walking in the bar smiled and replied, "Yah, gotta watch my figure, ya know." He said patting his stomach staining his belt.

Rick removed his sunglasses allowing his eyes' to adjusted from the bright morning Key West sun to the dimly lit bar and saw the usual morning bar patrons; "Three Fingers", "Ugly Larry", "Hooknose", "Stumpy", and "Two Tooth."

Rick saluted them saying, "Good morning, gentlemen."

Before she poured his beer, the morning bar tender at Che Che's Bar, a Key West local's watering hole, asked. "Did ya pay off yer tab yet?"

Rick's sun bleached hair, flowing from under a well-worn straw cowboy hat and wearing a white button down Columbia shirt yellowed at the arm pits and embroidered with "Seven Seas Charter" answered, "I think I paid something when Stevo asked. I had a good week and was celebrating, he wanted some money so I think I gave him some. But ya better check, don't wanna piss him off."

Ski, the morning bar tender with short florescent purple hair and numerous piercings in both ears, both eye brows, nose and her lower

34

lip pulled a ledger from beneath the bar to check. The manager, Stevo, said not to extend any more credit to the fishermen who inhabit the bar unless their tab was paid off. Her dark purple nail polished finger traced down the names until she found Nash, Rick. Then the finger took a right turn across the page and found the amount due column reading zeros.

"Yer good," she told Rick and grabbed a glass and held it under the tap.

Rick, sitting at the bar, took a long draw of the cold amber liquid and thanked Ski.

A voice came from the doorway. "I thought I'd find you here."

Rick looked in the mirrored back bar, not really needing to see who was speaking, he recognized the voice. He hadn't heard it in years, but he grew up sharing a bedroom with it.

Rick swiveled on his stool and addressed the man dressed in a light gray suit and blue tie printed with palm trees as he entered the bar. "Hello big brother, what brings you down to the bar at 10 o'clock in the morning?"

Rick's brother David was a lawyer in Key West specializing in divorce and family matters. In the last three years they had rarely seen one another.

"We have to talk," David said pulling out the bar stool next to Rick, his fingers coming away sticky. He wiped them with a monogrammed handkerchief.

"Dad is dead. I got a call yesterday," David said getting right to the point.

"No shit, the old man is dead, huh?"

Waving off Ski who placed a cardboard coaster in front of him, David answered, "Yes, and I was named as the executor of his will. He left the farm to you." David said placing some legal looking documents on the bar.

Rick picked up the papers, leafed through them briefly and said, "What did you get?"

"He left the balance of his bank account, the proceeds of his life insurance policy and his 401k to me."

"So you get all the cash and I get the farm, huh?"

"Yes," David answered and added sarcastically, "He knew how much you like living on the farm and left it all to you."

Rick downed his beer and motioned to Ski for another, "What the hell am I going to do with a farm in Michigan?"

"I don't know; work the land, or I guess you can sell it." David said.

"You know as well as me that the farm was mortgaged up the ass. It's got no value. How much did the old man leave you?"

David answered skirting the answer like a true lawyer, "Not much. By time I clear his credit card debt, it'll probably be less than a hundred grand. If that."

Rick raised his glass to his lips taking a sip, and calming down said, "So you get a hundred thousand dollars, and I get a fucking run down, worthless farm up in Podunk Junction, Michigan."

"It's not Podunk Junction, the farm is in Ubly, Michigan. Did you forget?" David got down from the stool and said to his little brother, "You need to sign this asset disposition document so I can file them with the court and make everything legal." David flipped to the last page and pointed to the line for Rick to sign.

David called to Ski, "Hey babe, would you come over here and sign that you witnessed Rick and I sign these documents. We want to make sure they are all nice and legal."

Ski signed where David pointed then left to get Ugly Larry another beer.

"Here's your copy. The farm is all yours."

Then before he left David added sarcastically, "I hope you have a good harvest."

Ski could see the expression of anger on Rick's beat red face and brought him another beer. "Who's the suit?"

Rick pushed the straw hat back on his head, took a long draw on the draft and replied. "That was my brother David, he just stopped by to tell me our dad died."

Ski, with a look of compassion placed a comforting hand on Rick's forearm, "Oh Rick, I'm so sorry."

Rick shook his head saying, "No big deal. I haven't seen the old man in probably twenty-five years. Not since he and my mom split. She wasn't cut out to milk cows and raise chickens. So one night she packed us up and we started over in Tampa."

"Now the old man ups and croaks and leaves my brother all his money and leaves me the farm. What the hell am I supposed to do with a farm in Michigan? I mean, do I look like a farmer to you?"

Ski smiled and said, "Hey, ya got the hat for it."

Sitting in his Lexus outside Che Che's, the air conditioner cooling the Key West morning warmth, David dialed his wife. "Did he sign it?" she answers.

"Yeah, and he never even asked to see the will. The idiot just signed and gave away his rights to all of the liquid assets. They're all ours. And poor stupid Rick is now the proud owner of some heavily mortgaged farmland in Michigan."

"Are you sure he can't come after the money once he finds out how bad the farm is?"

"Hey, I'm a lawyer. It's my job to make sure a contract is irrevocable."

It was over two thousand miles from Key West to the thumb area of lower Michigan's mitten, a three-day trip, Rick made it in seven. He set off in his twenty-two-year-old Ford F150. Two tires blew out before he reached Tennessee, parts of the trucks tailpipe are somewhere along I 75 in Ohio, and replacing the front wheel bearings maxed out his Visa, but he made it.

Rick stopped on the road in front of the farmhouse. It didn't look like he remembered. The white paint of the house was peeling with gray weathered wood showing through. The apple tree he remembered helping his dad plant had neither fruit nor leaves. The lawn his dad took meticulous care of was overgrown and infested with bright yellow dandelions.

He drove up the gravel driveway, pitted with potholes, and looked at the barn behind the house. He remembered it as red with white trim, now it was weathered with several boards missing and the door hung from one hinge. Around the barn sat various rusted farm implements, some with remnants of green paint and yellow John Deere logos. It had been a quarter of a century since Rick lived on the farm but he recognized the old Case IH field cultivator and Massey Ferguson combine.

The sight of the 1953 Farmall C brought back the memory of him as an eight-year-old learning to muck out the pig pens with the tractor. Now it sat in knee high weeds, rusty and corroding next to two other tractors each in worse shape than the Farmall. Rick thought, "David got a hundred grand and I got rust and weeds."

The chicken coop where Rick helped his mother gather eggs had collapsed and was just a pile of wood in a wire cage. The other out buildings were not in any better condition, the roof of the machine shop had caved in and sheets of metal siding were flapping in the breeze.

Looking around Rick realized the farm had not been worked in years, probably over in a decade. The equipment was decaying, the fields had gone fallow, the buildings not repairable.

In the house Rick found photographs of he and David hanging on the walls, but it was as if time had stopped. The photographs showed the boys from birth until their mother, frustrated with life, took the boys in the middle of the night and left. Leaving their dad only memories and a note saying she couldn't live the rural life anymore.

The kitchen hadn't changed; the sink was stained with rust streaks from the iron in the water. The living room furniture was the same too, wallpaper in the dining room was pealing from the wall and he noticed several brown stains on the ceiling where the roof was leaking. He looked around murmuring, "What the hell am I going to do with this place? The house isn't worth repairing, the land has gone to weeds, the buildings all need to be torn down and all the rusty shit in the yard is going to cost a fortune to have hauled away. I don't see any upside to this. I probably won't be able to sell it like it is, and I don't have the money to fix it up to sell it. I'm really screwed."

That evening after a dinner of a Big Mac, cold fries and a six pack, Rick sat in a ripped leather recliner, and wondered, "What the hell am I going to do? I maxed out my plastic getting here, I'm almost out of cash and I now I own a farm that is probably mortgaged up the ass. I'll be lucky to sell this place and have enough gas money to get back to the islands."

Rick jumped, startled by the ring of his phone. He pulled the phone out of his pocket and answered before the third ring. "Yeah?"

"Rick, it's David."

"What do you want? Got another inheritance for me?"

"Well, baby brother, it is about our inheritance, there seems to be a problem."

"What problem? How can it get any worse? Is the farm in foreclosure? Is it on a toxic waste dump?"

"No, it's the insurance and 401k. It seems years ago dad borrowed against the insurance and his retirement plan. There isn't any money in either account. We're going to need to work something out that is a little more equitable for each of us, we're going to need to share in the proceeds of the sale of the farm."

"Wait a minute. You're telling me that your share of dad's inheritance isn't as much as you thought so now I have to give you some of my share of dad's inheritance?

"We just need to renegotiate the disposition of the assets in a fair and equitable manner, in a way our father would have wanted. It's done all the time in inheritance dispositions."

"David, this is bullshit! I have a paper we both signed describing the disposition of dad's assets as was stated in the will. You get all the cash in his bank account, the payout from his insurance policy and all of the money in his retirement fund and I get the farm. It didn't say anything about, unless the insurance and retirement funds were not up to your expectations. David, go to hell. We farmers don't take kindly to you city slickers reneging on an agreement." Rick hung up.

"I may be stuck with a farm that hasn't been worked in years, land that won't grow a healthy weed, and a bunch of old rusty shit that I'll have to pay hundreds to have hauled away before I can sell the place, but dammit dad left it to me and its mine." Then he added, "Mine and probably a couple of banks."

"Hey Ski," Rick said walking into Che Che's Bar at ten twenty AM to join the early drinking crew. Heads turned and hands waved to the man who had left months earlier and one they thought they would never see again. "Rick!"

"Rick, you're back! What are you doing here. I thought you were some big rancher up in Michigan?" Ski asked.

"Farmer. In Michigan we have farms. Where you come from, they are called ranches, my Lone Star Sweetie."

"Alright, I thought you left to claim your inheritance?"

"Gimme a Bud and I'll tell ya all about it."

Over an hour and a couple of beers, Rick explained to Ski and the other morning patrons about his experience as a Michigan farmer.

"The farm was a real piece of shit, the house was in bad shape, there was all kinds of old farm equipment, ya know plows, combines, old pick-ups and shit just rusting in the yard and the buildings were all fallin' down. A real mess."

"Then my brother tries to cheat me out of the farm cause he didn't get as much money as he thought he was going to get, so I take the paper-work to a lawyer to have it checked out.

I picked one from the phone book and luckily it was the same attor-ney who did all my dad's legal stuff. He knew all about the farm."

"Dad hadn't worked the land in over 19 years and the land had all gone fallow. I think that's what it's called, anyway it was all overgrown with weeds and trees and the farming machinery wasn't any good no more. So I'm sittin' there in his office wondering how much he was going to charge me to tell me the place was worthless. Hell, I figured that out on my own."

Rick pushed his old straw hat up higher on his head and motioned to Ski to draw him another beer.

"Turns out my dad didn't need to farm the land because the govern-ment paid him not to. It was in some Federal agricultural land conser-vation program. I don't have to do a thing and each year I'll get a check from the government."

The group listened to Rick's story and cheered his good news. A hand, less a thumb and index finger, patted Rick's back.

Rick quiets his friends, "Hold on, there's more. A while back oil was discovered on the back section and there are five wells pumping so I get paid for them too." He quieted the group again to continue. "And on the east 80 acres some energy company put up a bunch of windmills, ya know those wind generator things, so I get paid for them being on the land too. With all of that I don't need to do a thing and I collect hun-dreds of thousands of dollars a year."

Rick's friends celebrated their friend's good news, Ugly Larry was dancing an Irish jig, Hooknose hugged Rick and Two Tooth was broadly smiling revealing the source of his moniker.

Rick shouted over the celebration, "Ski, drinks on me!"

Key West is a small island, only measuring two by four miles, and the news gets around quick, especially news of one of its colorful characters like Rick. It wasn't long before Rick's cell phone rang with a call from his brother.

"Rick, we need to talk. I've had dad's will reviewed by estate law experts and it was originally interpreted incorrectly. Turns out all the proceeds from the death of dad is to be divided equally between his remaining blood relatives; you and I."

"Ya know David, I had an attorney up in Michigan check the papers you gave me. By the way he was dad's attorney and drew up dad's will, something you failed to include in the stack of legal documents you gave me. And David, you're right, the will was interrupted incorrectly. It does state all of dad's assets should be divided equally between you and I. Nowhere did the document stipulate that you got all the cash, and I got the farm, we were supposed to share everything."

David said, "There, see that's what I'm trying to tell you. Dad wanted us to split the proceeds of his estate equally."

"But you said dad specified that you get the bank account, the insurance and the retirement, and that I inherited the farm. Yet in fact, the will was quite clear that we were to share equally in his entire estate."

David agreed, "I know, we share everything equally, little brother." Then David added, "I'm sorry, you didn't get a copy of the will, I had my girl, Bonita, copy it and she must have forgotten to include it. She's kind of a twit, always screwing up. But, anyway, now that it is all cleared up, come on down to the office and we can get everything equally distributed between us. I'll take care of the paperwork; you won't have to worry about a thing."

"But, David, there is one other thing."

"What's that?"

"David, remember those papers you had me sign? Well, that is a legal document. And in it you specifically stated that you receive dads bank account, the payout of dad's insurance policy and his retirement fund and I inherited the farm. It was clearly stated and signed by you and I and you even had Ski witness it, making it all legal. And according to my attorney, even though you accidentally interpreted ole daddy's will wrong, the other document we signed is perfectly legal and I don't have to share the farm with you."

"No, that's wrong. If you try to cheat me out of my legal inheritance, I'll sue the shit out of you!" David yelled into the phone.

"David, if you try to sue me it will come out that you violated your sacred oath, or whatever you lawyers have, in keeping the will from me and lying about what it said. Hell, my attorney says you'll most likely be disbarred and probably do some jail time for fraud too. Now get off my ass Big Brother."

"Sure, you're the expert, you're the smart lawyer, you know what you're doing, David's wife, Debra Sue, hollered at him. "You wrote a contract so binding that Rick couldn't weasel out of, made sure it was fool-proof, even had a witness sign it and now you pissed away the hundreds of thousands of dollars per year the farm will bring in. You are such an idiot!"

"Hold on, hold on, I've got an idea," David said trying to placate his ranting wife. What if something happened to Rick, like maybe he vanishes while he's out fishing. You know, falls over and gets eaten by sharks. And his last will and testament names me as his sole heir, then we get everything. Not just my half but all of it. What do you think?"

"Let me think about it for a second. It sounds too good to be true, too simple," Debra Sue says. "Does he have a will?"

David says, "Rick? Hell, before he inherited the farm, he didn't have anything to will to anyone. He could barely scrape up the money for his captain's license fee, much less pay a lawyer to draw up a will.

David continued, "I'll draw up a will and back date it sometime before dad died so it doesn't look suspicious. I can scan Rick's signature from the asset disposition document and insert it on the will. This will be easy. I'll do it here on my laptop and tomorrow I'll use Bonita's stamp to notarize it then sneak it into the file cabinet. Then when my little brother bites the dust we get it all."

Debra Sue said, "Perfect, now we just need to figure out how Rick dies."

Hooknose ran into Che Che's Bar, he had news, bad news, but he was pretty sure he was the only one who knew it and that made him important. Panting heavily from running more than he had in thirty years, without being chased, Hooknose sucked in a deep breath, reached for Stumpy's beer, threw back the last few inches and announced, "Rick is dead!"

The guys gathered around Hooknose, Three Fingers held him from falling, Two Tooth fanned him with a bar towel, Ski got him a beer and Stumpy held his glass to his lips, draining the last few drops Hooknose left.

"What are you talking about?" Ski demanded as she drew a draft for Hooknose.

Hooknose was panting and downed his shell in one gulp. "This morning, I was down by the old submarine pens, cause that's where I fell asleep last night and I woke up when the police and ambulance came cause someone found a body floating off the wharf. And I saw them pull out the body and it was Rick. It was Rick, our Rick. It was Rick. Rick's dead!"

The funeral was attended by a grieving brother David, Debra Sue pretended to be wracked in grief, Ski and the boys; "Three Finger", "Ugly Larry", "Hooknose", "Stumpy, and "Two Tooth."

After Rick's ashes were dumped into the harbor, David went back to his office to look up his poor dead brothers last will and testament.

The will, dated three and half years' prior to their dad's death, was a simple boilerplate document leaving all of Rick's earthly belongings to his only living blood relative, his brother, David Anthony Nash.

As the bailiff in probate court announced the case before Judge Cory that morning, Linda Main, the judges clerk of over twenty years excused herself and left the court.

The judge thought, "That's odd, Linda doesn't leave during proceedings, maybe she has another urinary infection."

David presented his brother's last will and testament to Judge Richard Cory, a graying and plump man tanned by the South Florida sun saying, "Mr. Nash, I'm sorry about your brother. I went out fishing with him a couple of times. He was a good man."

The judge was about to sign off on the probate documents when his clerk returned and placed papers on his desk. Judge Cory picked it up and looked over them.

"Seems we have a problem." The judge said looking at David. Then he read the document out loud.

"I, Richard Wayne Nash, of Key West, Florida having no former wills and codicils declare this to be my First and Last Will and Testament."

The judge paused to silently read that section again, "...having no former wills and codicils..." Then continued reading.

Article I
Identification of family

I am not married, nor have I ever been married.

I have no children, that I am aware of.

My only living relative is David Nash of Key West, Florida.

Article II
Payment of debt

I direct that my just debts, funeral expenses, and expenses of my last illness to be first paid from my estate prior to disposition.

Article III
Disposition of Property

Tangible Personal Property: All my tangible personal property shall be distributed in equal shares to the person or persons listed as the beneficiary of my estate.

The judge paused and flipped to the signatory page. "This is dated just last month." The judge held up the page to the light and adjusts his glasses to better read the notary stamp, "And it was notarized by court clerk Linda Main here in the courthouse."

"Mr. Nash, I am afraid the will your brother signed leaving the entirety of his estate to you is found to be invalid. I hereby rule the will you have presented is no longer current and has been superseded by the current document the has clerk provided."

The judge continued reading Rick's wishes, "I declare my estate be placed in a trust with bi-monthly payments from the Trust distributed equally between the named beneficiaries."

The judge flipped the pages to find the list of beneficiaries. "The beneficiaries are; Mr. Frank "Three Fingers" Namath, Mr. Lawrence "Ugly Larry" O'Leary, Mr. Bartholomew "Hooknose" Van Mutter, Mr. Randolph "Stumpy" Daniels, Mr. James "Two Tooth" Johnson and Ms. Melinda Sue Kowalski. All of Key West, Florida."

The judge then turned his attention to David. "Mr. Nash, your brother states here... "having no former wills and codicils I declare this to be my First and Last Will and Testament," emphasizing the word First.

The judge picked up the will and testament David presented to the court and asked, "Then where did this one come from?"

"Mr. Nash, I'd like to talk to you in my chambers."

"Mrs. Main, please contact the sheriff's office, I'd like to have a deputy join us in my chambers as well."

A STATEMENT OF UNREQUITED LOVE

Kasie and Chris had been waiting for this day. They were on a long overdue vacation in the Florida Keys. It was a warm February day; they rented kayaks at Robbie's to paddle out to Indian Key to explore the historic island. The island, part of the Florida State Park System, is only a few hundred yards south of the US 1 highway but it remains a few hundred years in the past.

Jacob Housman purchased the Indian Key property in July 1831 and built a hotel, warehouses, wharves, repair shops and a large house for himself. The island offered ocean breezes that were cooling and limited the blood sucking mosquito population and most importantly it had deep-water anchorage.

The settlement flourished and grew in population, even becoming the Dade County seat. The island's residents were employed in farming, sponging, fishing, turtling, salt and charcoal making, with the most profitable endeavor being wrecking, or the salvaging of ships, cargo and crews that had run aground on the shallow reefs. At the time navigational charts didn't exist or inaccurate at best, the square rigger ships were slow to the tiller and difficult to navigate, there were not lighthouses to warn of the reefs, and there was no way to forecast weather conditions and severe storms were frequent. Therefore, many ships ran up on the reefs and the wreckers raced to them to claim salvage rights. The salvers received payment based on the judgment of a wrecker's court.

Jacob Housman was one of the Keys most successful wreckers until 1840 when during the Second Seminole War, the Native Americans attacked and destroyed his settlement at Indian Key, the buildings were burnt to the ground. Many of the residents of the island were slaughtered.

Being such a rich historical area Kasie was eager to paddle the distance from Robbie's to Indian Key. Robbie's bait shop, boat rental and marina is located in Islamorada on the Gulf side of US 1. The couple negotiated the incoming tide under the US 1 Indian Keys Fill bridge and avoided the crowded island dock, instead followed the shoreline to a small opening in the mangroves. As Chris stepped out, he noticed something half buried in the sand. It looked like an odd shaped rock, upon closer inspection he realized it was a bottle.

"Watch out, looks like there is glass in the water, there's a bottle over here, he said to Kasie.

They both wore water shoes, never knowing what they might step on. Chris bent to pick it up, it resisted his pull, his index finger carefully dug around the object, expecting to pull out a jagged and sharp broken bottle. Instead, when he withdrew the object it wasn't broken. It was a complete bottle thoroughly encrusted with barnacles, mussels and other shellfish.

"Let me see it," Kasie asked.

Handing it over Chris said, "Careful, some of that crap is sharp."

Kasie turned it over several times looking at all sides of the bottle. "It's old. And it's been in the ocean for a while," she said as she placed it in the forward dry storage compartment of her kayak. "I want to take it home."

Back home in Savannah, their tropical vacation now just memories, photographs and charges on their credit cards, Kasie unwrapped the souvenir she brought back from their Indian Key kayak trip. On closer study of the object she could tell it was definitely a bottle under the layer of marine growth. A Goggle search and a quick drive to the closest marine supplies store and Kasie was ready to immerse the bottle in a plastic tub filled with an acidic barnacle remover.

After hours she put on rubber gloves and lifted the bottle from the bubbling cauldron. To her surprise most of the marine growth had been devoured by the solution. After scrubbing the bottle and a through rinse she dried it and began studying her treasure.

Turning it over in her hands, she could see the top of the bottle was a thick blob of glass with a cork broken off in the stem. The bottle had been rolling in the surf and sand for years rendering an almost sand blasted surface, she couldn't see into the interior of the bottle. The upper portion of the bottle seemed to be texturized, there was something embossed on the glass. With the aid of a magnifying glass and a bright light she could barely make out the figure that looked like a kneeling woman. Looking closer she mumbled to herself, "Hum, it looks like she has wings."

There might have been words embossed on the glass as well, but they were pretty well worn smooth.

On the computer, Kasie searched for antique bottles. A couple of hours later she was able to determine from the embossed woman the bottle was from the White Rock beverage company.

Wikipedia provided Kasie with an image of the kneeling woman, the Greek Goddess Psyche. She served as the company's logo since the late 1800's and appeared on all of the White Rock products.

When Chris got home Kasie was so excited to show him the bottle and tell him the history of the White Rock Beverage company. "I found bottles on the internet for sale on Ebay that look just like this one. See the embossed goddess and the blob top, those are signs that it is old. I think it is from the 1890's."

"Ebay? People buy stuff like this?" Chris asked. "How much are we talking?"

"Not much, ten to twenty dollars, that's all." Kasie responded. "For that much I'd rather keep it as a memory of our vacation."

Chris turned the bottle over under the light. "Too bad it's so cloudy; it would look better if you could see through the glass."

"Yeah, I know." Agreed Kasie. "Maybe we should pull the cork and see if we can wash the inside. See if that helps."

Carefully removing the old cork from the neck of the bottle became their project of the night. First, they tried the most obvious tool, a cork screw. Chris threaded the spiral into the cork and pulled. The corkscrew came out ripping the cork, not removing it. A pair of needle nose pliers reached in the opening pulled some loose material out but most of the cork remained. A screwdriver was successful in breaking the stopper into several pieces and forcing them down into the bottle.

Kasie turned the bottle upside down shaking out the loose cork pieces, then held it up to her eye to see if she got it all. "Chris, I think there is something else in here. I think it's a piece of paper. It's a note in a bottle!" Kasie screamed in excitement.

With the help of a pair of forceps from Chris's Physician Assistant college days, they carefully pulled the rolled piece of paper through the neck and out the blob top opening. Wearing latex gloves Kasie slowly unrolled the brittle piece of paper on the granite kitchen counter.

"Chris, look there's writing!" It was faint but mostly still legible.

Chris brought the magnifying glass and the bright desk light.

Kasie began reading.

August 28, 1887

My love, Miss Anna Belle Covington, has found another. I hereby remit my love for her to the sea. I shall never return home again to evade the pain of seeing my beloved in the arms of another.

She shall forever remain a part of my heart.

John Anderson

Boatswain's Mate, 2nd Class

USS Maine

Kasie wiped a tear running down her cheek and said, "The poor guy was heartbroken. He was aboard a ship, probably away for months or years at a time and his love found another. Imagine the pain of his loss. And to ease the pain he wrote this letter and threw his love for Anna Belle into the ocean. Oh, Chris, this is so romantic."

"Yeah, a real Hallmark movie. I bet the bottle is worth more now that we found a letter over 120 years old in it."

Kasie playfully punched her husband in the arm, "I'm never getting rid of this. I need to figure out how to preserve the note."

Within a week Kasie had done a search for Anna Belle Covington. The search turned up nothing. Although a search of John Anderson provided how he died and where he was buried.

One day her husband called from work. "Chris, I found out a lot about John Anderson!" Like it says on the letter he was on the *U.S.S. Maine*. On February 15, 1889 the *U.S.S. Maine*, the most powerful ship the US Navy fleet, was in Havana Harbor when it exploded. Over half of its crew, 260 American sailors, died in the blast and resulting fire. It was suspected that the Spanish bombed the US Navy ship. The destruction of the ship and the rallying cry of "Remember the Maine" provided President McKinley the justification to declare war on Spain."

Chris interrupted, "Hon, that's all very interesting, tell me the rest when I get home. Do you need anything for dinner?"

"Get a pizza, I'm too excited to cook, Kasie responded.

Chris no sooner walked in than Kasie was reciting facts about the *U.S.S. Maine*.

"Do you know where our John Anderson is buried?"

Chris popped the top on a beer and asked, "Our John Anderson? Have we adopted him?"

"Yes. I have spent so much time studying him and for over a hundred years the bottle with his letter of unrequited love floated around the ocean and we found it. It's almost like he found us. I feel very close to him, and I want to visit his grave."

"Kasie, I think we have spent enough time and money on this. The guy threw a note in a bottle off his ship, a note in which he says he is throwing away his love for that Anna woman. He was ending it, now you need to end your obsession with him and his story"

"Are you sure you don't want to visit his grave? He's buried in Key West," Kasie said, knowing her husband's love of the southernmost city.

They checked into the Key Lime Inn, quaint accommodations not far from the cemetery. Chris suggested a nap, but Kasie was anxious to get to the *U.S.S. Maine* monument.

They walked to the entrance of the cemetery at the northwest corner of Passover Lane and Angela Street.

Kasie told her husband all she knew about the historic Key West cemetery. "An 1846 a hurricane destroyed the cemetery and since the bodies were buried in shallow graves the storm scattered the dead about the island. It was rebuilt in 1847. Now most of the bodies are buried above ground in Crypts, some are marked with unusual and humorous tombstones. "One woman had her stone engraved with, "See, I told you I was sick." Another read, "I'm just resting my eyes."

He reminded her that they were not tourists taking the cemetery tour that they came to pay their respects to John Anderson.

Kasie switched tracts to give Chris a running commentary of what she had learned of the explosion onboard the ship and the internment of its victims.

"After an investigation of what caused the explosion, the navy determined the battleship struck a mine submerged in the harbor triggering the ship's ammunition bunker to explode." Kasie continued, "However, many questioned that finding. They say the ship used a type of coal that was susceptible to spontaneous combustion, and some theorize a coal fire set off the ammunition explosion, thus the ship was not sabotaged."

"It happened in Havana, Cuba," Chris stated, "Why is John buried in Key West?"

Kasie answered, "The first victims recovered were buried in the Colon Cemetery in Cuba, although most of them were later reburied in Arlington National Cemetery in Washington D.C.. In fact, the rear mast from the ship serves as the memorial there. Some bodies that could be identified were sent to their families for burial. The remains of twenty-four other sailors who were found later were sent to Key West for a burial. Key West is only 90 miles from Havana, and it was the last port of call for the *U.S.S. Maine*."

As they entered the cemetery off Angela Street, Kasie unfolded a map of the cemetery she downloaded. "There it is," she said pointing.

"Where?"

"See the monument with a statue of a standing sailor holding an oar and shielding his eyes as he looks out to sea."

As they slowly and respectfully approached the monument Kasie looked down at the flowering orchid she carried and said. "I'm nervous. Ever since finding the bottle, cleaning it, discovering the note in it, sharing his pain of unrequited love and spending so much time researching Boatswain's Mate, Second Class John Anderson I feel I know him. I feel he is a part of me."

The couple stood before the monument, reading the inscription etched in granite:

IN MEMORY OF THE VICTIMS OF THE
DISASTER OF THE U.S.S. BATTLESHIP "MAINE"
IN HAVANA HARBOR
FEBRUARY 15, 1898.

Chris knelt to dig a hole for the white orchid they brought as an offering to John Anderson's memory. He broke the soil with his motel key then dug with his fingers. Two inches down he struck a hard object. He used the key to dig around it.

"What is it?" Kasie asked.

Concentrating on his task, Chris answered, "I don't know probably a rock."

Digging out dirt he loosened, Chris exclaimed, "Oh my god, I think it's another bottle."

He continued digging while Kasie looked around waiting to be arrested for disturbing consecrated ground or grave robbing or something.

Finally, he withdrew another White Rock soda bottle, like the one they found in the ocean off Indian key, this one minus all the marine growth.

"It's got a cork in it," Kasie exclaimed.

Looking through the smudged dirt on the glass Chris added holding the bottle up to the sun, "Yeah, and it looks like a note inside too."

"Here, stick it in your purse. We have to take it back to the motel and see if we can open it."

Kasie asked as they quickly walked, "What do you think is on the note in the bottle? Is it another of John Anderson's notes about the love of his life, Anna Belle? Or just maybe it's a note from Anna Belle." She continued to postulate as they walked the mile back to the Key Lime Inn. "Maybe after John died, she made a journey down here to his grave with an apology for breaking his heart."

The front desk was able to provide a corkscrew but they said they would need to chase down the maintenance man for a screwdriver. As they walked by the pool they found Javier cleaning the pool filters. They practically ran in excitement to their room, a screwdriver and needle nose pliers in hand and the mystery bottle in Kasie's purse.

Sitting on the bed, Chris followed the same procedure as in the past; corkscrew, pliers, screwdriver. This cork had not spent a century in the ocean, it was not as fragile as the other.

"You know we can always break the bottle open," Chris suggested.

"No, keep trying. The bottles are part of the story. I'd like to keep it whole. And it might damage the letter inside."

Kasie poured herself a glass of wine and got Chris a beer. As he broke small pieces of cork away with the screwdriver and extracted them with the pliers. Two beers, two glasses of wine and nearly two hours later the cork fell into the bottle. Without the forceps to withdraw the paper Chris tried to grab it with the pliers and Kasie's tweezers with no success.

"I need a break," Chris announced. "I'll check with Javier maybe he has an idea." He grabbed a beer from the mini-fridge and stepped outside.

Kasie looked at the bottle and said to herself, "Maybe we should just break the damn thing." She picked up the bottle and tried to get her little finger in, her fingertip just missed the roll of paper. In frustration she shook the bottle several times. When she looked at it, to her amazement the paper had shifted. It was further up the neck of the bottle. Her finger could just touch the paper. She twisted her finger rolling the paper into a tighter cylinder. She slowly withdrew her finger and the paper came too, then slid off. But the paper was in reach of the tweezers. She slowly pulled the paper out.

Kasie held her breath as she unrolled the note. Would it be a love letter for Anna Belle, or one from her? Was it a note John Anderson wrote as he laid dying on the burning *U.S.S. Maine*?

She read the note written in the same ornate script as the first letter.

Chris entered the room to find his wife sitting on the bed. He could tell she had been crying. Then he saw the bottle lying next to her. It was empty. The rolled piece of paper lay next to it.

"You got it!" Chris yelled. "You got it out!" he reached for the paper, carefully unrolling it. He read;

"I hope you enjoyed your treasure hunt. Bring this note to the Hibiscus Grill at 926 Simonton Street, Key West, Florida and you will be rewarded for your

perseverance, effort and determination in solving this puzzle. You will receive a free beverage with the purchase of any dinner."

Kasie was the first to break the silence. "I bet someone found an old encrusted bottle, stuck a note in it and placed it where we found it. After all Indian Key is very popular with kayakers, making discovery of the bottle almost guaranteed."

Chris added, "Yeah, and human curiosity did the rest. Whoever set this whole thing up knew that the finder, namely us, would become so entrenched in the love story, the history of the *U.S.S. Maine* and the lure of Key West that we would go to great lengths and expense to pursue the lives of John Anderson and Anna Belle Covington."

"Son of a bitch!" Chris said.

Kasie replied, "Yeah, son of a bitch!"

After a calming and soothing swim in the pool and a few drinks Chris said to Kasie, "Come on let's get ready and go to the Hibiscus Grill for our reward dinner."

"I'm not going there," Kasie shot back.

"Hey, someone went to a lot of trouble to perpetuate this hoax. Now we have to follow through and complete it."

Kasie and Chris took a table at the Hibiscus Grill.

"Hey how y'all doing?" The waitress with a Tammy name badge over her left breast greeted them.

Chris laid the rolled paper on the table asking if she knew anything about it. Tammy's eyes opened and she said, "Oh, ah, I'll get the boss."

A man with gray hair almost as greasy as his white apron came from the kitchen, wiping his hands on a towel. "Hi, I'm Grant. What can I do for you?"

Kasie took the lead, "Grant, we found this in an old bottle. Do you know anything about it?" She said lifting the paper to him.

The man, perspiration beaded on his forehead from working over the stove read it and smiled. "I'll be damned. You found it. I told the professor no one would ever find it. That he was just wasting his time."

Chris said, "Wait, who's the professor?"

"When I first bought the place there was an old guy who hung around here, ate most his meals here in fact. He said he used to teach at FSU, that's why we called him the Professor. Anyway, he told me that years earlier he threw some bottles in the ocean with clues in em."

"We found the first bottle off Indian Key, and it had a note in it." Kasie told him.

"Grant motioned to Tammy to bring water."

"The Professor used to sit at that table over there and wait for someone to bring in one of his bottles." Grant pointed at a small table near the door. "Almost every day he would come in and ask me, "Do you have any mail for me?"

"Ya know you're the first to ever bring one in. The old professor would be a happy man knowing someone found it."

"Is he still around?" Kasie asked.

"Naw, he died a while back, buried in the cemetery near the Maine memorial."

Kasie gave her husband a look, and repeated, "Near the Maine memorial."

Chris asked, "Do you know how long ago the Professor put the bottles in the ocean?"

Grant took a big gulp of his ice water as he thought. "I think he said he threw them in when he retired and as I recall that was about twenty-three years before I bought this place. The old owner joked that I bought a restaurant and a professor."

"So he put the bottles in the ocean twenty-three years before you bought the Hibiscus Grill and, how long ago was that?" Kasie asked.

"Forty-eight years ago come this August."

"The bottle was floating in the ocean waiting for us to find it for 71 years!"

Grant called Tammy to the table and said, "Honey, give these fine folks a free beverage with the purchase of a dinner."

ONLINE DATING

"Hey, Bubbles."

"Hey, Brock."

The same salutation they had exchanged each workday for the last three years. Brock is the 38-year-old day bartender at Lorelei's Restaurant and Cabana Bar in Islamorada, and Bubbles actually is 28-year-old Britney Shirk, known for her bubbly personality and a favorite of the wait staff.

The Lorelei is located bayside at mile marker 82 on US 1. Its thirty-foot-tall mermaid welcomes all, locals and tourists, young and old, rich and poor, and the famous and infamous. They come to enjoy the nightly live entertainment, some of the best seafood in the Keys and fantastic sunsets. The marina offers charter fishing boats, pirate ship tours, a motorized floating tiki bar, kayak rentals and even the world famous floating pink Cadillac, NautiLimo.

Brock could tell Bubbles wasn't her typical vivacious self. She usually kidded with Brock, playful banter between co-workers, but not today. Today after a customary, "Hey, Brock." She silently prepared for her shift. Through the shift Brock noticed that Bubbles who usually took the customers flirtations with a funny, but keep your hands off response, but when a semi drunk regular made a snide reference to her ample bosom, she slapped him across the head. Brock noticed, she hit him hard, it wasn't a playful slap, it was a good solid smack.

As the lunch rush slowed and just a few locals were left inhabiting the bar stools Britney walked to the bar to place a drink order. Brock asked, "Hey Bubble's, you okay?"

She pushed back a hank of hair that had escaped from the scrunchie creating a ponytail. With sweat beading on her forehead a testament to the heat of the tropical island she answered, "Yeah, I'm okay. Just a little down today."

Later Bubbles and Brock took their break together and he asked again, "Hey kid, what's up? You're not you today."

"I got a text last night from a friend from high school. She got engaged and next week they are driving down to Key West, she wants to stop by so I can meet her fiancée."

Brock for the last three years has been Britney's coworker, partner in work place practical jokes and her shoulder to cry on. He helped through the death of her grandmother, bailed her out after a DUI, held her hair back as she vomited, and comforted her during a couple bad breakups. They were great friends, both accepted each other for who they were; she could stand to lose a few pounds and maybe do something with her hair and she didn't notice any longer that his head was a bit misshapen and scarred, and his right eye looked in a different direction than the left, the result of a past motorcycle accident.

Bubbles complained, "Sue never even dated in high school and now she has a fiancée. I don't have a fiancée. Hell Brock, I haven't even had a date in months! It's like life is passing me by."

"Bubbles have you tried an online dating service?" Karen, another server at Lorelei asked.

"No, maybe I should. The way I've been meeting guys hasn't worked out so good for me. Of the three guys I dated seriously since I moved down here; turns out Brent was gay, Tom disappeared one step ahead of his creditors and good old Jeff was married. And I'm sure you remember the scene when his wife showed up here. Maybe I should try a dating service."

Diane offered, "Honey, I've tried them all, the one I'm using now is called, *Pen Pals: Who They Are, Not How They Look*. I like it cause it's free and there are no names or photographs exchanged. You set up a contact name and a profile. The computer picks guys that have similar interests, then you scan through them. When you find one of interest you send him a chat request using the Pen Pal website. He guy doesn't have a way to see who you are, he doesn't know where you live, unless you give him your personal information. It's all private. What you're supposed to do is get to know the other person first through chatting before you meet."

"Has it worked for you?" Bubbles, a bit susceptible, asks.

"I've met a couple nice guys, no one to introduce to my mama, and I've met a couple real losers. But, I have a couple of guys I'm still writing, ya know getting to know them, taking it slow."

Sitting on her bed, the laptop on her lap, Britney opened the *Pen Pals* website. She stared at the page hesitant to take the first step, then she remembered Sue's text about being engaged and pushed the SIGN IN tab.

After skimming a several-page long contract, she pressed, I AGREE, then was asked to create a personal contact name; minimum six characters, including at least one upper case letter and a minimum of one number. She decided on a name she could easily remember; "Bubbles906", her nickname and the area code of her hometown in Michigan. Next, she began to answer the basic information questionnaire; name, sex, age, hair color, eye color, nationality, geographic location, profession, height and weight. She was sure most people fudged their answer on that last one, her answer chopped 10 pounds from reality.

The following section requested her preferences in a dating candidate; age, sex, race, nationality, sexual preference, profession, height, weight, hair and eye color.

Not being picky she answered and quickly pushed SEND before she backed out.

"Hey Bubbles!" Brock said as he she walked in and he was wiping down the bar.

"Hey, Brock. It's a beautiful day in the neighborhood."

"Yes, it is. I'm glad to see you're your same old self again."

"Yup, I decided to take the plunge, grab the bull by the horns, take control of my own destiny." She raised her clenched fists high and said, "I am my own woman!"

Brock laughed and shook his head; he was glad Bubbles was back.

Throughout the shift Bubbles filled in Brock on her foray into the mysterious world of online dating.

"It was easy, and most importantly it was free." He listened as he drew another Yuengling draft for a sunburned tourist sitting in the shade at the bar.

Bubbles picked up four beers and a mimosa for table 8 and told Brock, "I checked before I came in and I already have three notes, that's what they call it when someone writes you."

On the next trip to the bar she said, "Now I just need to decide which of them I want to respond to. Oh, and give me a rag, I just spilled beer on that lady who is way too old for her tight pink tank top."

A few days later Brock greeted his co-worker. "Hey Bubbles, How's the dating going? Ready to meet any of them or are they still just Pen Pals?"

"Hey, Brock. Yeah, I'm writing some guys. A couple of them have potential! Keep your fingers crossed."

Later she told Brock she was almost ready to meet one of her notes. "He's a guy named, "Buck22" We've been writing for a couple of weeks, he sounds nice. Kind of a jock, he said 22 was his number when he played wide receiver in college. That's football, isn't it?"

Sitting on her bed in a Key Largo tee shirt and gym shorts, laptop on her lap Bubbles read the latest note from Buck22.

Buck22: *"We've been writing a while now, over two weeks, I think. When are we going to meet?"*

Bubbles906: *"Two weeks and three days, to be exact. I know I've been taking it real slow and it's probably time to go a meet, but this is the first time for me and I'm nervous."* She wrote, having the same self-deprecating thoughts that plagued her since elementary school; "What if he thinks I'm too fat, or that I'm ugly, and a dummy."

Buck22: *"If you don't want to do a meet in person, how about we exchange pictures? Then at least when I lay in bed at night dreaming of you I can put a face to my fantasy girl."*

Bubbles906: *"You're too sweet. Buck22, what if I don't stack up to your fantasy girl? Let me think about it. Good night."*

She opened the next note with a topic line, Pen Pal has a Hit for you; Micky414 has written.

Micky414: *"Hi Bubbles906. I'm Micky414. I read your profile and I think we have a lot in common. Would you like to write and get to know each other? I have to confess I'm new to all of this online stuff."*

Bubbles906: *"Hi Micky414. I'm new to this online stuff too. I find it rather intimidating."*

Micky414: *"Yeah, me too. I'm sort of a shy guy to begin with. How has this Pen Pal thing worked out for you? Have many meets?"*

Bubbles906: *"I've been chatting with a few guys, but no meets. How about you?"*

Micky414: *"Just chats. To be truthful you're only the second person I've chatted with."*

Bubbles906: *"Micky, let's chat some more at another time. I've got to get to bed, work tomorrow."*

Micky414: *"Yeah, me too. I look forward to chatting again. Good night Bubbles906."*

Bubbles906: *"Good night Micky414."*

"Hey Bubbles."

"Hey Brock."

"How's the dating thing going?"

"Running late, we'll talk later. In fact, I need some advice."

"We should have time, gotta storm coming in. It'll be slow."

When the rain came the customers left. An open air, waterfront restaurant just didn't have the same appeal when the sky turned gray and opened up with torrents of rain.

Brock wiped the bar down as Bubbles cashed out her last customer. "So, how can I help you?" he asked.

"Brock, it's this whole dating thing. I have I guy I have been chatting with and we get along really good. He is easy to communicate with and we seem to have a lot in common. Now he wants to take the next step and do a meet. A meet, that's what Pen Pal calls it when two people graduate from chatting to meeting. But, I don't know if I'm ready for it."

Brock smiles and asks, "Do you want to meet this guy?"

"I do, but what if he doesn't like me? What if he thinks I'm too fat? What if likes blonds and I only have this ugly brown straw?" She says running her fingers through her hair.

Brock responds, "That's enough with all the negative "What if's". The only "What if" you need to worry about is, what if he is the one?"

"But what if he isn't? she asked.

"There you go with another negative "What if." If he isn't the one then screw him, he is missing out on a great girl."

One evening, sitting on her bed in her old Manistique Emeralds tee shirt, Bubbles held her breath and wrote.

Buck22: *"Okay, let's do a meet."*

As Bubbles walked into the bar Brock said, "Hey Bubbles. You're early."

"Hey Brock, I did it! I agreed to meet Buck22. I'm so scared."

"Where, when?" Brock wanted to know. "Some place public I hope."

"Yeah, here. I'm doing a meet with the guy tomorrow, on my day off, here at Lorelei. You're working, aren't you? I was hoping you would keep an eye on me. Ya know, sorta make sure the guy isn't some deranged rapist or serial killer."

"I'll be here, I'll be checking him out for you."

"You're so sweet, Brock." She said giving him a hug. He was such a sweetie she no long even noticed his imperfections, like the eye that scans the sky while he looks at you.

The next morning Britney was a wreck. There was a pile of clothes on her bed she had pulled from the closet and drawers, tried on and vetoed. She didn't know what to wear. She looked in the mirror, sucked in her stomach saying, "That didn't help much." She dragged a brush though her hair, wishing she had got it cut and maybe some highlights. "Why did I agree to a meet? This guy is a big college jock. I never even went to college; I'm going to disappoint him. I'm going to embarrass myself."

As agreed on Bubbles sat at one of the tables near the stage and close to the beach, wearing a lime green blouse and jean shorts and sipping a Tequila Sunrise to fortify her for what she thought would be a predictable miserable experience.

Brock winked at her and reassured her that she looked great and not to be nervous.

A few minutes later Buck22 walked in, looking for a lady in a lime green top. He introduced himself and sat down across from Bubbles.

He ordered a beer, and they talked for twenty minutes. They rose, he gave her a friendly hug and kiss on the cheek, they promised to keep chatting, he left, and Bubbles went to Brock watching from the bar.

Brock slid another drink to her, knowing how anxious she was that she might need it. "So that was Buck22, huh? The college wide receiver? I bet he wore a leather helmet when he played. How old is he anyway?"

"I don't know on his profile it said he was 54, a little older than I planned on dating, but from the looks of him I think he was closer to 74." She and Brock had a laugh, not at Buck22, but at how nervous Bubbles was, afraid she would disappoint her meet, never considering that she would be the one disappointed.

"Did you see his hair?" Bubbles asked. "It was a terrible dye job and when he leaned in for the goodbye hug I saw some duct tape under his shirt, probably trying to pull the wrinkles out of his neck." They laughed again, this time at Buck22's expense.

Over the course of the next month Bubbles chatted with several guys on Pen Pal. There was ACTionguy3, 100%Hunk, Chris18 and she still chatted with Micky414. She arranged for a meet with the first three at the bar under the watchful eyes, well one eye of Brock, his other eye watched the ceiling fan.

From his contact name, ACTionguy3, and their chats Bubbles thought he was a man of action, some kind of superhero. Rather he was an actuary by profession, hence ACTionguy3. After the introduction and usual meeting pleasantries he began talking about being an actuary and never stopped until they departed. Bubbles learned that he was responsible for the measurement of risk and uncertainty for an insurance company. He stressed his importance that it was he who controlled the bottom line of the company's balance sheet. He was in control of the company's asset management and liability management. He proudly declared, "If it weren't for the actuarial scientists the world's economy would crumble."

Bubbles was glad the Meet ended early because ACTionguy3 had to get back to work.

Her next date was with 100%Hunk. She should have known by his name, but she had a weakness for bad boys. She entered the bar, thanked

Brock for the rum and Coke and sat at her "Meet Table" as she and Brock came to call it.

100%Hunk did not disappoint; he lived up to his name. Bubbles was uncomfortable about her weight in the presence of a guy who obviously worked out regularly. She said, "I've been meaning to get into the gym and lose a few pounds". And he responded, "Yeah, you could stand to lose a good15 to 20 pounds, but you're still doable."

She paused, not believing what she heard. She thought, "Did he really say I was overweight but still DOABLE?"

She got up and politely said, "Fuck you!" and walked away. She resisted the urge to dump her drink over his head. She walked to the bar for Brock console and protect her.

Her date with Chris18 went well. They both had a Tequila Sunrise and talked easily. Bubbles was less intimidated because Chris was a little on the heavy side too. He wore his hair in a short cut, spiked with gel. He said he just got out of the army, moved to the Florida Keys and was looking for work in the hospitality business.

Bubbles enjoyed her time with Chris18 but the brief hug as they departed confirmed her suspicion. When they hugged Bubbles felt breasts pressing against hers. Bubbles went home to double-check that she had checked the right boxes on her profile questionnaire.

After her failed Meet experiences, she laid off Pen Pal for a while, only chatting occasionally with Micky414 who never made a request to do a Meet. They were friends, someone to spend time with. She once told him how much she enjoyed his attention and responded he looked forward to chatting with her too.

It was Bubbles who suggested they do a Meet. Micky414 was hesitant but finally agreed. Bubbles suggested her usual Meet Table on Friday at noon. He agreed.

Friday morning Bubbles found she wasn't nervous like she was with the other dates. She dressed without emptying her closet, she calmly walked in Lorelei, waved at Brock and ordered a Tequila Sunrise.

Brock delivered her drink and sat down across from her, there was time before her guest was to arrive. They laughed about some of Bubble's disastrous past meets and he wished her better luck this time around.

Bubbles checked her watch then said, "Brock, you better get going, I don't want to make Micky414 jealous."

Brock smiled, one eye staring at her the other at the clouds and said, "Bubbles, my name is Michel James Brockway, I was born on April 14th. I'm Micky414."

NATURE CALLED

Will Mellard is a serial killer who is crisscrossing America practicing his own brand of selective elimination. He seeks out people whom he determines are a menace to society. Specifically, people who take pleasure in hurting others; wife abusers, child molesters, white collar criminals who destroyed the lives of their employees, sometimes he kills people just because he doesn't' like them, and in a twist of irony, Will also murders murderers

On a beautiful sunny day, Will was driving a rented red Mustang convertible down US 1 towards Key West. He was admiring the view from the Seven Mile Bridge; the Gulf of Mexico on the right and the aqua blue water of the Atlantic to his left. He drove with one hand on the steering wheel while the other was turning on his cell phone to take a photograph. Concentrating on pressing buttons, he was startled when a white Cadillac suddenly came up on him fast from behind blaring its horn.

Will quickly looked up from his phone to see he had veered left and was straddling the center line taking up both north and southbound lanes, fortunately, there wasn't any oncoming traffic. He quickly moved to his lane and the Cadillac swung out to pass. The driver floored his car to emphasize his anger. Will looked left at the car with an apologetic expression. But when the white Cadillac with a New York license plate and a New England Patriots bumper sticker flew by, Will saw the man giving him the finger.

"That son of a bitch scared the shit out of me. Screw you, asshole!" Will shouted, shaking his fist with a raised middle finger as the white car disappeared in the distance.

Will checked the rear-view mirror and finding no other vehicles behind him slowed down again to take in the tropical paradise of the Florida Keys.

In Key West, Will partook in all of the normal tourist activities, drank a beer at Sloppy Joe's and Hog's Breath, ate a cheeseburger in paradise at Margaritaville, and took a ride on the Conch Train. He had heard about the sunset celebration held at Mallory Square each evening and was anxious to join that party like atmosphere.

As he walked down Duval Street towards the waterfront, Will stopped to look in the store windows selling anything from 3 for $10.00 tee shirts to gallery quality art, from dope smoking paraphernalia to diamond jewelry. He listened to live music blaring from the open-air establishments, and he was amazed to see people walking down the street openly carrying cups of beer.

At Mallory Square, where the cruise ships dock and regurgitated thousands of tourists onto the small island, Will found street performers setting up for the evening's sunset celebration. He sat on a bench and settled in to do some people watching and drink the beer he picked up at Captain Tony's Bar.

Mallory Square was beginning to fill with people, many wearing Royal Caribbean or Carnival Cruise Line stickers on their shirts, families from all around the country, and couples and individuals of all ages. There were college students; many of the guys had obnoxiously consumed to excess and the girls paraded around wearing the minimum. There were middle-aged people, some acting and dressing as though they were re-living their younger years, and foreign tourists snapping pictures of the chickens and roosters freely roaming the city streets. However, it seemed to Will that the Baby Boomer generation represented the largest segment of the tourist population.

The beers had swelled Will's bladder to the point he needed to seek relief. He asked a City of Key West municipal worker emptying a trash can where the restrooms were.

The man pointed to a small building near the main entrance to the square. "See them people standing over yonder? That be it."

Will looked at two lines snaking down the sidewalk. The line of men was long, and the women's line was even longer. "I don't know if I can wait that long," he mumbled.

The man laughed and said, "Know what ya mean brother, when nature calls ya gots ta answer. Not suppose to tell ya, but there's private johns beyond them bushes. They're for the construction crew workin' on the new hotel. But the gate in the fence looks locked but it ain't. I use em all the time."

Will thanked the man, tossed his empty cup in the trash and walked toward the row of deep red bougainvillea.

As he approached the parking lot Will noticed a car straddling the painted parking lot line taking up two spaces. It was a white Cadillac just like the one that blew by him earlier that day. He checked and it had New York plates and the same bumper sticker. The driver who flipped him off was sitting in the air conditioning yelling at someone on the other end of his cell phone. Will's anger at the man began to once again boil.

The so-called private toilets apparently not so private. Will watched a family of tourists open the gate to use the private portable toilets. The driver of the white Cadillac also entered. Will followed the man through the gate to a row of four functioning blue plastic portable toilets and one with an out of order sign.

Will, the family and Cadillac Man were the only people in line for the currently occupied facilities. One member of the family of four stood in front of each unit waiting for the red occupied signs on the doors to turn to green, reading unoccupied. Will stood in line patiently waiting his turn thinking of the time he and his mother went to the Missouri State Fair and his mother called these types of toilets "Plastic Poop Palaces."

An older woman wearing a tight-fitting Schooner's Wharf Bar tee shirt, short cutoff jeans. Dishwater blond hair flowing from a straw cowboy hat and boots walked out of the larger handicapped porta john. The young boy standing next in line, squirming in obvious urinary distress, started in but Cadillac Man suddenly stepped in front of the boy and entered. Will watched and was pissed, and nothing ever good comes from pissing off a serial killer.

The door opened in the plastic cubical Will was next in line for, but he motioned the boy to take his turn. Will stepped to his right to wait outside the handicapped unit.

The family completed the tasks at hand and departed the area of the "Plastic Poop Palaces," leaving only an asshole in the handicapped unit and an angry serial killer waiting outside it.

When the little sign changed to unoccupied and the door began to open, Will rushed in taking the man by surprise.

A few minutes later Will opened the door and exited. He took the out of order sign taped to the door of the defective toilet, stuck it on the handicapped unit and walked back to Mallory Square to watch a man balancing on a unicycle while juggling flaming batons.

The next morning several cars with flashing red and blue lights and an ambulance whose attendants didn't seem to be in a hurry filled the new hotel parking lot. Key West Police officers had encircled the portable toilets with yellow crime scene tape holding back twenty to thirty tourists snapping pictures to post on their Facebook pages. Among the group was the serial killer, Will Mellard.

When the medical examiner arrived, she approached an officer and asked, "So, what do we have?"

"Dead guy in the handicapped portable toilet," he responded.

"Who was first on the scene?" she asked.

"I was," he responded.

"Did you attempt resuscitation?" the M.E. asked.

Writing notes of the crime scene in his small notebook he responded, "Huh? What? I didn't hear you."

Not pleased to repeat herself, she asked irritably pronouncing each word slowly and precisely, "Did you give the victim mouth to mouth resuscitation?" she asked.

"Hell no!" he replied emphatically.

"Why not?' she said admonishing the cop. "Department policy states the first officer to respond at the scene of a person in distress must make an attempt to resuscitate the victim."

With a gloved hand, the officer opened the door of the handicapped portable toilet. She looked inside seeing a man with his head shoved down into the disgusting mixture of blue deodorizing liquid, urine, Tampons, soggy toilet paper and shit.

The medical examiner said, "I think we can rule out suicide."

THE YELLOW JEEP WRANGLER

2001 Jeep Wrangler Sport, 5 speed manual, Yellow, black soft top, no rips, 6 cylinder, interior good, no rust, lift kit, tires new a year ago. 149,800 miles, A real Keys Cruiser! $5,000. Cash only.

Daisy Texted her friend Mitchel. *"I found my car!"*
Mitchel: *"Cool. When RU going to look @ it?"*
Daisy: *"Wed. morn."*
Mitchel: *"@ work call later."*

Daisy has been waiting tables at upper Keys restaurants and taking classes at the Florida Keys Community College since she graduated from Coral Shores High School two years earlier. She had been driving the old Taurus her dad gave her, but she was saving to buy a Jeep Wrangler.

She knew some kids from high school who drove Jeeps, and she fell in love with the 4-wheel drive vehicles. She remembered driving to Key West in Billy Albury's red Wrangler. Five of them in a four-passenger car. The top was down, and Billy took the doors off. It was so cool. Driving down US 1 sitting in the back with Karen and Kate while Mel and Bart were in front. Her blond hair flowed in wild tangles and the girls stood holding onto the roll bar and sang with the radio blasting as they crossed the Seven Mile Bridge.

Daisy was so excited, soon she would have a Jeep, and she'd put down the top down and take off the doors too. And it was yellow, her favorite color.

Mitch has been her best guy pal since third grade when they met on the playground. He was being teased by some of the boys and she stood up for the new kid. Twelve years later he was still being teased and she still had his back.

Daisy was anxious to talk to Mitch, to tell him all about the car, to plan some beach trips with the top down. Maybe they would go to Key West and drive her Key's Cruiser up and down Duval Street or maybe go up to South Beach.

The meowing growl of an angry cat, her cell ring tone, interrupted her fantasy about showing off her yellow Jeep.

"Mitch, I can't believe it. It's in my price range, it's still available, and its yellow!"

"Where is it?"

"The guy lives down on Grassey Key, but he is going to drive up on Wednesday morning and we're going to meet at the Indian Key Fill, mile marker 79, at 10 o'clock."

"Oh, Daisy, I don't think that's a good idea. You're always supposed to meet strangers when you're buying stuff online at a fire station or a police station. Ya know someplace where there are people around to watch you. Someplace safe."

"Mitch, you're such a scaredy cat. There are a lot of people at the Fill. Ya know it's a place where locals and people from Miami fish from the shore, swim and picnic. There are tons people all over."

"But not on a Wednesday morning. You're going to be carrying a bunch of cash. The guy could show up in the yellow jeep stick a gun in your face, take your $5,000 dollars then drive away."

"Then you come with me. You be my backup. My protector against all things evil."

"I can't I gotta work Wednesday morning. I'll try to get off, but I already know what my ass of a boss is going to say."

"Okay. Hey, I gotta call coming in, it's Bonnie. I left her a message about my new Jeep. I bet she's jealous."

Tuesday evening at work Mitchel lifted a box of frozen all beef patties and pulled a muscle or something. The pain went down the left side of his neck into his back. The manager saw it happen, he couldn't accuse Mitch of faking it and suggested he take Wednesday off.

He called Daisy to let her know he could go with her to pick up the yellow Jeep.

Mitchel drove Daisy to the Indian Key Fill in his baby blue Mustang convertible. She teased him because he had a stiff neck and couldn't look side to side. As they drove, she opened her purse a couple of times to make sure the bank envelope with her life savings was still there. Passing the entrance to Tea Table Key they saw the yellow Jeep parked ahead nearly hidden from the road by the mangroves. Mitch approached slowly and stopped saying, "It's like he is hiding. I don't like this." But Daisy ran from the car towards the yellow Jeep. As agreed, Mitch stayed in the car to keep an eye on the transaction.

Two guys in a pickup truck pulled in off the highway to launch their flats boat. They blocked Mitch's view. He pulled ahead so he could keep an eye on Daisy. She was excited walking around the car checking it out and talking to the guy in a gray hoody. "I don't like this at all," Mitch thought. "It's too warm to wear a hoody. I bet the guy has a gun in his belt under the sweatshirt. He's going to pull it and steal Dasie's money!" His imagination was getting the best of him.

Mitch opened the center council and pulled out his dad's pistol he took from his house. He fired the Glock .44 a couple of times and knew how to use it. Mitch sat in his Mustang, the pistol in his lap and watched Daisy and the guy. Daisy opened her purse and took out the envelope filled with five thousand dollars. The man in the gray hoody reached his right hand behind his back.

Mitch jumped out of his car, the Glock pointed at the guy in the gray hoody and yelled to Daisy, "Gun! He's got a gun."

The guy in the hoody pulled his hand from behind his back with the title to the jeep, the men launching their boat, two off duty Monroe County Sheriff Deputies pulled their off-duty weapons, took aim at Mitch and yelled, "Put your gun down!"

His stiff neck not allowing his head to turn, Mitch turned at the waist. As his body turned so did the hand holding the Glock 44 pointing it at the deputies. Three shots rang out, one shattered the windshield of the baby blue Mustang, two others hitting Mitch. He collapsed to the ground. Daisy's protector lay dead at the Indian Key Fill.

OUT OF CHARACTER

Sitting in interrogation room 3 at the Monroe County Sheriff's Department substation in Islamorada were Deputy Radak and Deputy Lynn Jefferies, they had been called to the Holiday Inn for a domestic dispute and brought Leonard Demoski in for questioning. Deputy Radak asked; "Mr. Demoski, can I call you Leonard?"

"Naw, call me Lenny, everyone does. Leonard was my father."

"Lenny, we need to talk about your wife."

"Yeah, that's what I thought. What ya want to know?"

The deputy started off with simple questions to develop a relationship with Lenny. "Well, let's start with what brought you to the islands?"

Lenny smiled and happily told the deputies "Marcy and I are Queener's. We're here for the annual convention.

"Queener's? I haven't heard of Queener's before."

"Yeah, we're an organization of devotees of the 1951 John Huston movie, *African Queen*. Queener's, get it?"

"Ah okay. So, your annual convention is here in Key Largo?"

"Yup, It's at the Holiday Inn. It's sorta our Mecca. It's where the boat is. You do know that the *African Queen*, the actual boat used in the movie is docked by the Holiday Inn. Its where we Queener's come to pay homage to The Queen. This year we have a 33% increase in attendance! It's a new record. The turnout is amazing. We've got 15 Queener's from the US and even a guy from Canada. We've gone international!"

"We all dress up like Humphrey Bogart and Kathrine Hepburn did in the movie. But since they wore the same costume throughout the entire movie, it's not as exciting as it sounds. We all look alike. Marcy grew her hair out like Hepburn's, and had it colored and styled, she was a shoe in to win the lookalike contest."

"I've never seen the movie," Deputy Jefferies said.

"You're kidding! The movie was a huge success, the top money-maker of 1951, and it earned Bogey an Oscar for Best Actor in a Leading Role."

Lenny is quick to begin telling the African Queen neophyte the story line. Deputy Radak let him talk, figuring it will help them develop a rapport with Lenny and gain his trust and hopefully his cooperation.

"It's the best movie ever made. It takes place in 1914 in the Congo during the beginning of World War I. A couple of British Christian missionaries; the Reverend Samuel Sayer and his sister Miss Rose Sayer, that's Kathrine Hepburn, are there to convert the people to Christianity but the German imperial troops burn down the village and kill Reverend Sayer. The only way for Rose to get to civilization is on the run-down river boat that ferries people and supplies, the *African Queen*, captained by a Canadian, Charlie Allnut. That's Bogey."

"Now, the prim and proper Rose Sayer considers Charlie Allnut a little rough around the edges, he is gruff, he curses, and he is a drunk."

Deputy Jefferies asks, "What kind of boat is the *African Queen*, like a sailboat or a cabin cruiser or something?"

Lenny with a look of astonishment asks, "Girl, you live in the Key's, and you've never seen The *African Queen*?"

"Nope."

"You've got to stop some time, it's at mile marker 100 on US 1 ocean-side. She's an open-hulled, 28 foot, wood boat powered by a steam engine. She's over 100 years old, ya know."

"Anyway, the movie is about Rose and Charlie and their journey on the river. Mr. Allnut wants to find a cove and hide from the German Gun boat in the area, but Rose decides they should attack it to seek revenge for her brother's death."

Deputy Radak interrupts, "Hey Lenny, give us the abbreviated version, we don't have all day."

"Okay. Anyway, they go through rapids and got stuck in the reeds and Bogey has to get out and pull the boat to deeper water and gets leaches all over his body."

"Abbreviated version, Deputy Radak reminds Lenny."

"Yeah, they make it through the river and into Lake Albert where the German gunship is and they rig up a torpedo and plan to ram the German boat and sink it, but it doesn't work, and they get captured and German captain says they're going to be executed. The dialogue between the German captain, Rose and Charlie is fantastic. On the journey Rose and Charlie fall in love and they ask the captain that before they are executed if he would marry them."

Deputy Jefferies said, "Aw, it's a love story."

"Yeah, sorta."

The German captain asks: *"What kind of craziness is this?"*

Then Charlie says: *"Aw come on, Captain, it'll only take a minute, and it'll mean a lot to the lady."*

The captain says: *"Very well, if you wish it absolutely. What are your names again?"*

Bogey says: *"Charles."*

Rose says: *"Rosie. Rose."*

The captain says: *"Do you, Charles, take this woman to be your lawful wedded wife?"*

He says: *"Yes, sir."*

Then the captain says: *"Do you, Rose, take this man to be your lawful wedded husband?"*

And Rose says: *"I do."*

"Lenny says, "Now this is a great line. The captain says," *"By the authority vested in me by Kaiser Wilhelm II, I pronounce you man and wife. Proceed with the execution."*

Deputy Radak again interrupts, "Okay, okay. Enough of the *African Queen*. Lenny tell us about Marcy, what happened yesterday?"

"Okay. Well, let's see, we got up about 8:00 and had breakfast around the pool. I had pancakes, two eggs, sunny side up, I don't like that slimy stuff on the egg so I had it done over easy. I was going to order bacon, but Marcy said I gotta start watching my cholesterol. I remember Marcy was going to order the French toast but changed her mind and got eggs Benedict. She didn't like it. She's never had it before; I think she just ordered it because it sounded fancy. Ya know, acting all proper like Miss Rose."

Deputy Radak said in frustration. "I don't care what you had for breakfast! What did you do after you ate?"

Lenny cocked his head to the side in concentration, "Well, we had reservations for a tour on *The Queen* but that wasn't till 10:30 so we walked around the grounds for a while then went back to the room, Marcy had to poop. That's Marcy, always has to poop after a meal. She says as soon as she puts something in it wants out. I know too much information. Let's see, then we changed into our Rose and Mr. Allnut outfits."

"The ride on the boat was fantastic. Marcy and I have dreamed of taking the tour on the boat since it was announced on the Queener's website the convention was in Key Largo this year. The captain topped off water in the boiler, ignited the firebox and as it heated up there was hissing steam rising from the vent and with a spin of the flywheel the old engine comes to life. With its putt, putt, putt sound just like in the movie. And the captain blows the steam whistle, man, it was music to my ears."

"Marcy looked so pretty sitting on the port side all prim and proper, wearing her wide brim hat, just like Rose's, to shield her from the sun. Her hair all up just like Hepburn, she was the spitting image of Rose Sayer. I took a bunch of pictures on my phone. And I was wearing my Charlie Allnut outfit. I found a hat just like his in a thrift store, white with a black brim. And I had my scarf around my neck just like him and I was wearing the shirt I had custom tailored to exactly match his. We looked spiffy, I tell ya, spiffy We sat back just like we was in the Congo going down the river back in 1914."

I start saying dialogue from the movie, It's the scene Marcy and I were going to do at the convention talent show. This just after Rose and Charlie shot the rapids;

"I don't blame you for being scared, Miss, not one little bit. Ain't no person in their right mind ain't scared of white water."

Then Marcy says: *"I never dreamed that any mere physical experience could be so stimulating!"*

"How's that, Miss?"

"I've only known such excitement a few times before - a few times in my dear brother's sermons when the spirit was really upon him."

"You mean you want to go on?"

"Naturally."

"Miss, you're crazy."

"I beg your pardon."

"You know what would have happened if we would have come up against one of them rocks?"

"But we didn't. I must say I'm filled with admiration for your skill, Mr. All-nut. Do you suppose I'll try practice steering a bit that someday I might try? I can hardly wait... Now that I've had a taste of it. I don't wonder your love of boating, Mr. Allnut."

"That's very good." Deputy Radak said, "But we need to talk about your wife."

Deputy Jefferies interrupts, "Oh, no. I want to hear more."

Lenny ignores Deputy Radak and launches into another bit of dialog.

"Ooooh! Coward yourself! You ain't no lady. No, Miss. That's what my poor old Mother would say to you, if my poor old Mother was to hear you. Whose boat is this, anyway? I asked you on board 'cause I was sorry for you on account of your losing your brother and all. What you get for feeling sorry for people! Well, I ain't sorry no more, you crazy, psalm-singing, skinny old maid!"

Deputy Radak looks at his watch and in frustration says, "Okay, that's it, Lenny, enough about Boggy and Hepburn, we need to talk about your wife."

"Yeah, I was sorta getting there. After our voyage on the *African Queen* we had lunch around the pool, my cheeseburger was to kill for.

And Marcy had a salad. She is always eating rabbit food trying to watch her figure. Trying to stay as thin as Hepburn, ya know. We had a few drinks too. Well for me it was a little more than a few, I sorta get sloshed, whiskey does that to me. "Ya know Bogey was a whiskey drinker. In fact, while filming in Africa, the entire cast and crew came down with dysentery except Bogey and the director. They never drank the water; all they drank was Scotch whiskey and never got sick."

"Then we went back to our room and Marcy took a nap and I had a couple more gin's over ice. Ya know in the movie Charlie had a case of gin on board. After one night when he got really snockered, he woke up to a glug, glug, glugging, splash sound."

Deputy Radak almost yells, "Lenny get to your wife. I'm tired of all this movie stuff."

"I am. I'm getting to my wife." Lenny said with a pleading expression. "Just give me a minute for some background information."

"Anyway, Charlie is really hungover, the sun is really bright and hurts his eyes, he can't make sense of the sounds. His eyes squint open and he sees Rose pulling the corks from his gin bottles, pouring them over the side and then throwing the empty bottle in the river."

Lenny slips into character and quotes Charlie: "*Oh, Miss. Oh, have pity, Miss. You don't know what you're doing Miss. I'll perish without a hair of the dog. Oh Miss, it ain't your property.*"

Lenny continues, "Now in the movie Charlie leans out over the side scooping the muddy river water into his mouth, trying to salvage some of his gin. Then he sits back in realization that all of his gin is gone. Rose never says a word.

"Get back to Marcy!" Deputy Radak says impatiently.

Lenny looks at the deputy and resumes, "Well, like I said I had a few drinks at lunch and then a few more back in the room, Marcy was yelling at me for drinking too much, then I sorta fell asleep, well I passed out. And I woke up to a glug, glug, glugging sound like Charlie Allnut did. It was Marcy pouring my gin down the toilet!"

"I said, "*Oh, Miss. Oh, have pity, Miss. You don't know what you're doing Miss. I'll perish without a hair of the dog. Oh Miss, it ain't your property.*"

Now in the movie Charlie in his drunken hangover sat back and sulked because Rose poured out all of his gin, I sorta came out of character, I was trying to get my gin back before Rosie, I mean Marcy, emptied the whole bottle and in my drunken state I pushed her. A little too hard apparently. She fell, her head hitting the bathtub. And that's why I'm here, for killing my wife, my Miss Rose Sayer."

THE BUOYANT BRA

Three college students, Darrel, Tommy and Will, had driven non-stop from Madison, Wisconsin to celebrate Spring Break in the fabulous Florida Keys. Seeking sun and sand, the guys went to Smathers Beach to relax and watch the parade of people strolling on the shore. The walkers were mostly wearing swimming attire and carrying Publix plastic bags to hold the collection of shells they picked from the sand at low tide.

"Ah, Spring Break, the annual pilgrimage of the youth of America to the sun and warmth of Florida," Darrell, the philosopher of the three said as he lay on his beach towel, watching young nubile nymphs frolicking in the warm surf and down the beach spiking a ball over a net. "Hey guys ya want to play volleyball?" Tommy the "Jock" of the three asked his friends.

"No, not me," Will, the ever cautious one responded. "The soft sand doesn't support your feet properly; you can easily break an ankle."

"Come on let's cool off in the ocean," Darrel suggested.

"Yeah," Tommy said, getting up and flexing for anyone who might be watching.

Will responded, "Here? There isn't a lifeguard. It wouldn't be safe; we would be swimming at our own risk. What if there is a rip tide and we get sucked out to sea?"

"Okay," Darrel said. "We will just walk in up to our knees and wade in the water. How's that?"

Will, asked, "What about sharks? Are there sharks in the water? Or stingrays? It was a stingray that killed the naturalist guy, remember?"

Tommy, getting a bit irritated with their paranoid friend responded, "Of course there are sharks, it's the ocean!" Then figuring Will would never go near the water added, "But I don't think there are any here because all the people would scare them off."

Darrell and Tommy walked into the water feeling the surf washing against their sun warmed legs. Darrell bent down to splash water on his shoulders to cool the sunburn he would later regret.

Will stood at the edge and asked, "Do you see any jellyfish?"

"No!" Tommy and Darrell said in unison.

Just as Will was taking a first step into the ocean, he heard a scream down the beach then a woman yelled, "Stingray!"

A crowd, including Tommy and Darrell, formed near the woman to watch the graceful creature skim across the sandy bottom. Will retreated to his beach towel twenty yards from the water.

The guys convinced Will that he had nothing to fear, there were hundreds of people on the beach and even small children were playing in the water. "At least come walk the beach with us," Darrel pleaded. Will finally agreed after Tommy called him a pussy.

The three guys joined the parade of locals, tourists and snowbirds walking along the beach, they even picked up shells, putting the keepers in their swimsuit pockets and throwing others back to the sea.

"Hey, what's that?" Darrell said, spotting something floating offshore.

"Where? I don't see anything," Tommy asked while Will stopped and backed away from the water.

Pointing, Darrell said, "It's about twenty feet offshore. See it?"

Will, with a hand shielding his eyes, scanned the surface and asked, "Is it an eel? A jellyfish? Maybe a Portuguese Man-O-war? They've been seen in these waters. They sting and I read its really painful."

Darrell took a few steps into the water to check out his discovery.

In a voice laced with urgency Will said, "Darrell be careful, jellyfish tentacles can be 10 feet long and they can sting you even though you're not near them." Will continued, "They can inject you with venom from thousands of microscopic stingers on the tentacles. It's painful and you can get really sick and sometimes even die from the stings. Darrell come back in," Will pleaded.

Getting tired of Will's paranoia, Darrell took small steps, closing the gap between himself and the mysterious object.

"Ha, it's not an eel, a jellyfish or a shark, It's a bra. Someone lost their bra and its floating on the surface. Guys, it's just a bra!"

Tommy started walking out and suggested, "We should walk the beach to see who the bra fits, sort of like Cinderella's glass slipper, only better!"

Just as Darrel got within reaching distance of the undergarment, Will yelled, "Darrell don't touch it! Don't go near it!"

Darrell pulled his hand back and asked Will, "Why not? It's just a bra."

The ever cautious yet paranoid Will replied, "Just step away from it. Don't touch it. Whatever you do. Don't touch it."

Tommy and Darrell again replied in unison, "Why? It's not going to hurt us."

Will with genuine fear in his eyes answered, "But, guys, it's a booby-trap!"

A WIZARD OF OZ MOMENT

"Fluffy. Fluffy." Sue scanned the backyard from side to side and from the deck to the lagoon. She whistles and resumes calling, "Fluffy. Fluffy. Come on dog, don't make me come out and get you.

Sue Johnson and her husband Bob had just retired and didn't want to spend another winter in Wichita. They found the Big Pine Key rental house on Airbnb and booked it for a month. Tiki lights lit the backyard but since Fluffy wandered off Sue went back in the house to search for the switch for the backyard flood lights. Unfamiliar with the house she flipped switches on and off, lights in various parts of the house flashed until the backyard was illuminated by flood lights.

"Fluffy. Fluffy. Come on girl." She listened but the small white Havanese didn't come running.

"Bob! Come help me find Fluffy," she yelled to her husband.

Putting down his Bud Lite and searching for the button on the unfamiliar remote to pause his movie he mumbled, "Damn dog. She cares more for the dog than she does for me."

"See if you can find a flashlight," she yelled.

The second kitchen drawer he pulled out produced a 1,000 lumen LED light. He looked at the lens as he pushed the button. Bad idea. Bob blinked his eyes from the bright light. "There goes my night vision, but the light works."

Bob stepped off the deck and found Sue walking in the backyard towards the lagoon, her phone in flashlight mode and yelling and whistling.

"Bob, you go that way, and I'll go this way."

Walking through neighbor's yards Bob wondered if someone is going to call the police on the strange man wandering around at 9:30 at night, or worse come out shooting. He turned around and could barely see the light of Sue's phone.

He returned to search for Fluffy. He shone the light back and forth and called the dog's name. Up ahead the flashlight illuminated something. He couldn't quite make out what it was. Fifty yards later he could make out the object was a sign at the edge of the lagoon. "I'm walking to there and turning around." He told himself. "Sue is probably already back at the house laying on the floor letting the damn dog lick her face."

He reached the sign, scanned the ground beyond it for the missing K-9 and turned around. He shined the light on the sign curious what it was for. "Probably a sign warning trespassers will be shot."

He turned his light to the sign and read:

CAUTION CROCODILES

American Crocodiles are known to inhabit the lagoon.
  Take Caution and follow these rules

- Absolutely No Swimming!
- Crocodiles prey on small animals. Avoid walking dogs and cats within 10 feet of the water's edge.
- Crocodiles are most active from dusk to dawn.
- Do not feed the crocodiles. It is illegal and when fed crocodiles lose their fear of humans and become a nuisance.
- Do not discard fish scraps into the lagoon.
- Do not feed ducks, fish, turtles or other aquatic life in the lagoon, it attracts the crocodile.
- It is illegal to kill, harass, feed, or possess a crocodile.

"Shit! Fluffy probably was an appetizer and Sue's walking by the lagoon, she could be the main course!" Bob turned and ran towards his wife, "Sue! Get away from the lagoon! Crocodiles!"

Bob had to stop to catch his breath before he dropped over with a coronary or his lungs burst. As he stood bent over, hands on knees, panting and perspiring, he heard Sue calling his name.

"Bob! Bob, I'm at home. Come home! Fluffy is here."

Without the same urgency Bob walked the rest of the way home. He found Sue standing holding Fluffy tightly and talking with an elderly lady.

"Bob, this is Wendy Talsma, Fluffy was over at her house."

Wendy warned the couple new to the Keys, "You have to be careful around here. There are crocodiles living in the lagoon and they eat small animals. Some days you can see them sunning themselves on the shore."

"Why don't they get rid of them, just kill them?" Bob asked.

An environmentalist at heart, Wendy said, "Well, for one thing the crocodile were here long before we were, this is their natural habitat. Back in 1975 the crocodile population was down to just a few hundred and was added to the endangered species list. Now the crocodile population is over 1,500 but still classified as "Threatened." They are an endangered species success story."

"Wendy, thank you so much for retuning my lovable ball of fur. I just let her out like we always do in Wichita I didn't know there were animals out here that want to eat my baby."

Bob, still out of breath retrieved his beer, joined the ladies and said to his wife, "Sue, I don't think we're in Kansas anymore."

AN ATTACK OF NATURE

Sitting back in the lounge chair, the vast expanse of the Florida Straits before him, an extra dry martini in hand and Maui Jim sunglasses blocking the bright sun, Vinny Azalone said to his wife lounging next to him, "This is the life. I'm so glad we bought on Sugarloaf Key."

Doreen shook her gold bracelet down her arm and picked up her white wine replying, "I know, I never want to leave. I love it here, away from the traffic of Atlanta, away from the hassle, away from work."

Relaxing in their seaside retreat after finalizing the purchase agreement earlier that day Vinny replied, "I know, it's our own little private hide away. And when the remodel is completed, and you work your magic on the landscaping it will be just the way we want it. It will be our Shangri-La, our Xanadu."

They clink their glasses toasting their new oceanside home.

"What's that!?" Doreen yells, pointing at a large lizard sunning itself on a boulder size piece of coral along the shore. "What is it? It looks prehistoric."

Lifting his sunglasses to get a better view, "I'm not sure. Some kind of lizard."

"The realtor didn't say anything about four-foot-long lizards roaming the property. I don't like this. I don't like it at all. The creature is scary looking. Do they bite?"

"I don't know," Vinny said looking around for a weapon to defend them from the beast."

Doreen yelled, "Vin look, its shaking its head up and down and it's got like a wing or something hanging from its jaw. Is it getting ready to attack?"

"I don't know." He slowly gets up to retrieve a rock lining the concrete patio. "You keep an eye on it. If it attacks, scream."

"Vinny, do you really think you need to tell me that. I'm going inside until that thing leaves."

"Yeah, that's probably a good idea."

They watched the reptile from the safety of their home, two layers of hurricane strength plate glass separating them from the prehistoric creature. "What should we do?" Vinny asked. "It's just sitting there, like its ready to pounce."

"I don't know. No one told us there were man eating lizards here," Vinny said looking at the creature through binoculars. "I bet it escaped from a zoo or circus or something."

"Or Jurassic Park. Well, I'm not going to be a prisoner in my own house, trapped by some prehistoric reptile. I'm going to do something about it," Doreen said, dialing 911 on her cell.

Vinny watched her explain to the 911 operator about the monster prowling their property.

Vinny asks, "What did they say? Are they sending out a unit to kill it?"

Doreen said disgustedly, "No. I told them about the creature roaming our property and then the line disconnected, we must have got cut off."

"Well, I know what to do," Vinny said as he walked to the bedroom. Minutes later he returned, he had removed his shorts, tee shirt, and sandals and put on long jeans, a long sleeve shirt, socks and shoes. As an afterthought he tucked his pant legs into the socks. "No use taking any chances, he thought. "That creature could run up my pants leg and bite my nuts."

Opening the front door cautiously just a couple of inches, he looked left then right making sure there wasn't a battalion of lizards mounting a frontal assault. He reached out his right hand with the car remote to unlock the doors, he didn't want to spend any more time than necessarily exposed to the horrible creatures. He ran to his car, his head swiveling side to side searching for any sign of the enemy. He practically dove in the driver's side and slammed the door. Scanning the ground around the car he was content none of the lizards had seen him race to the car. Vinny opened the console and took out his Beretta M9A1 pistol. He checked the pistol making sure it had a full clip. "Alright, you fucking dinosaur, now I'm ready for you."

Vinny leaned up over the dashboard looking out the windshield and side windows, checking for any invaders waiting for him to make his mad dash from the car back into the safety and security of his house. Seeing nothing he quickly opened the door and raced to the front door. On the run he reached back pushing a button and locking the car. On the porch he reached for the doorknob. "Shit!" he screamed. In all of his preparations to retrieve his armament he forgot to unlock the door. Frantically pounding on the door he heard from inside Doreen ask, "Who is it?"

"Me! It's me! Dammit Doreen, open the door before it gets me!"

Doreen hesitated to wonder if she really should open the door but after more pounding she unlocked the door. Vinny quickly slid in the door, opened just enough for him to slide in, slammed it shut and leaned against the door breathing heavily. Doreen stood a few feet away in running shorts, a hooded sweatshirt cinched tight around her head, wearing gardening boots and wielding a broom and steak knife for protection. She reset the security alarm.

"Vinny, what are we going to do? I won't sleep knowing that that monster is out there."

Vinny reached into his pocket and pulled out the pistol, held it up and said in his best Rambo voice, "I'm gonna take that son of a bitch out."

Vinny looked out the sliding glass doors, the beast was still there sitting in the sun on the coral boulder.

"Stand back Honey." Vinny opened the door enough to get his hand and the pistol out. With a shaking hand he took aim at the reptile and squeezed the trigger. The shot was high and made ripples in the ocean ten yards out. Vinny took aim again, wishing he had bought the optional laser scope. He squeezed off two more rounds, one far left the other to the right. His next shot struck the boulder with coral chips flying and the lizard scurried off into the Bougainvillea.

"Shit! He took off. But I might have nicked him," Vinny said.

Doreen said, "But it's still out there. That ugly scaly thing is still out there. I bet there are more. I'll never be able to enjoy the patio; I can't work in the gardens. That's it, we half to sell the house. I will never come here again!"

A knock at the front door interrupted Doreen's complaining and Vinny's search of the yard. They turned to the front door and through the windows they could see flashing red and blue lights.

Doreen exclaimed, "They're here! The police came to save us!"

Vinny walked towards the door, gun still in hand saying, "The 911 operator must have traced your call before you were disconnected. Thank God they are here."

Vinny swung the door open, a deputy yelled "Gun!" and two sharp prongs shot into Vinny's chest. He fell to the floor in uncontrollable convulsions.

The deputies explained to Doreen that her husband was under arrest for discharging a firearm in a populated area. He would be taken to the Lower Keys Medical Center in Key West for evaluation after being tased and then booked in the county jail on Stock Island.

Crying, Doreen tried to explain that they were under attack and Vinny shot at the creature in self-defense.

"Ma'am, the monster you are describing is a Green Iguana. They are all over south Florida. They're pretty much harmless, they only eat plants and don't attack humans. In fact, some find them quite delicious."

ROAD RAGE

Shane Tyme piloted his custom ordered bright yellow 37' Beneteau 373 Oceanis, named *Party Tyme*, off the Atlantic into the Snake River bridge approach. He had to steer carefully to avoid the two shallow reefs on either side of the entrance, but the calypso music blaring from the sound system, the bikini clad women dancing on the deck and the days' worth of rum and Coke didn't help his navigational skills any.

By order of the United States Coast Guard, the bridge at mile marker 86, opens only on the hour for vessels too tall to sail under the Whale Harbor Chanel bridge to the south or the Tavernier Creek bridge to the north. The bridge is a single-leaf bascule bridge connecting Plantation Key and Windley Keys in the village of Islamorada, the last remaining draw bridge in the Keys.

Waiting for the top of the hour, Shane had to maintain a light touch on the throttle with enough forward momentum to counter the current trying to push him back. Red lights on the bridge began to flash, traffic lane barricades lowered, cars and trucks in each direction came to a stop, and the bridge started to slowly rise. In his state of inebriation, he found the boat creeping forward. He was moving forward too fast, at this pace the bridge wouldn't be open enough for him to sail through, his mast would strike the steel structure of the bridge snapping it in two and potentially doing damage to the bridge, the only way for highway traffic to get from the upper Keys to the lower Keys. It would be catastrophic, the thousands of locals and tourists below the bridge couldn't get back to the upper Keys or the mainland and locals, tourists, food, beverages and other vital supplies couldn't be delivered below the bridge.

Seeing the collision was eminent, at the last moment, Shane swung the wheel hard to port, the sailboat, slow to respond, began its turn. Shane held his breath, praying it would turn before it struck the bridge. Bob Marley singing *One Love* blasted from the speakers while the half-drunk beauties on the forward deck continued to dance completely oblivious to the potential disaster before them.

Shane exhaled as *Party Tyme* came about missing the bridge by what seemed inches. Now he had to power back towards the Atlantic for a wide enough area to turn around and make another attempt. The wheel, hard to port *Party Tyme,* slowly came around. Shane pushed the throttle ahead to move quickly through the Snake Creek so the bridge could lower and the cars and trucks could continue on their way up and down Highway 1. But, sailboats don't move very fast.

It took so long for *Party Tyme* to make two attempts to get through the bridge the traffic on the Overseas highway was backed up for eight miles to the north and almost six to the south. Horns blared their displeasure of having to wait for the boat while dancing drunks on the deck waved at the stopped traffic.

Hunter Tyson sat in his pickup truck, eyes flared as the yellow sailboat with dancing girls held up traffic on US 1, the main road through the Florida Keys. He thought to himself; "The sailboat picked 5:00, the height of rush hour, for the bridge to open was bad enough, but the damn boat missed on its first try and had to turn around and try again."

He pounded the steering wheel with a fist saying, "Damn it, get that fucking boat going, I gotta get to work!" He laid on his horn and a girl in a skimpy lime green bikini making wild yet seductive gyrations to Marley waved at him. He flipped her off. She just laughed.

"What? What do you mean my boat is on fire?" Shane screamed into his cell. "I'll be there as soon as I can."

Shane drove the thirty-eight miles from his home to the Snake Creek marina in less than thirty minutes. He passed cars wildly on the 18 Mile

Stretch and did almost 65 in the 45 MPH area of Key Largo. Unfortunately, the Snake River Bridge was up for an outbound sailboat. Shane had to sit on US 1 watching the flames, flashing lights of the emergency vehicles and firefighters paying out hoses and spraying down *Party Tyme* docked at the Snake Creek Marina.

Chief Salvador Talarico explained to Shane that they tried to salvage *Party Tyme* but it quickly became apparent that it was going to be a total loss and they had to shift their effort to saving the other boats in the marina. *Party Tyme* settled to the bottom, only its mast stood above the surface like an invitation to an aquatic pole dancer.

The chief explained that a boat fire that spreads as quickly as it did on *Party Tyme* can only be caused by an accelerant of some kind being used. Someone intentionally set *Party Tyme* on fire.

The marina webcams had been tampered with and didn't record the person who set the fire, but a deputy checked the webcams at a nearby motel and they clearly showed a man in a dark colored hooded sweatshirt throw something on the boat, toss a flare into the cockpit and it instantly erupted into an inferno. The surveillance camera caught the image of a man running from the blazing boat, the left arm of his hoodie on fire. He ran frantically patting the flames on the sleeve. The image of the fire was sent to Jacksonville to be digitally enhanced.

Two days later the image was sent back and a copy was forwarded to all law enforcement officers in the Keys and asked to see if they could identify the perpetrator. Three deputies who worked the upper Keys all said they were certain the person the motel camera captured was Hunter Tyson, a bartender at the Green Iguana.

The deputies went to the home address of Hunter Tyson. There was a pickup in the drive. Make, model and license all matched that on record for Hunter Tyson. A knock on the front door was unanswered. The second knock, or rather a pounding, resulted in a voice from inside yelling, "Just a minute."

The door opened revealing a 28-year-old man, scruffy 4-day growth on his chin. The man was dressed in cargo shorts and a long sleeve Guy Harvey tee shirt featuring a sailfish breaking the surface a hook in its mouth.

"Yeah? What ya want?"

"Are you Hunter Tyson?" the deputy asked knowing full well it was.

"Yeah, that's me."

"Hunter, we want to talk to you about a fire down at Snake Creek Marina."

"I read about it in The Island Times, but I don't know any more about it?"

"Hunter do you know a man named Shane Tyme?"

"Nope, doesn't sound familiar. Why?"

"His boat was set on fire and burned and sunk four days ago."

"That's too bad."

"Hunter what were you doing about 1:30 in the morning last Thursday?"

"Sleeping. I'm not much of a night owl."

"You weren't at the Snake Creek Marina?"

"Hell no. Why would I be there?"

"Maybe to set Mr. Tyme's boat on fire?"

"I told ya I don't know no Mr. Tyme."

"A surveillance camera at the Lime Tree Motel showed you at the marina dousing the boat with something and igniting it."

"It wasn't me. I was in bed."

"But Hunter you were identified by several police officers as the man on the security tape."

"Nope, not me, they musta made a mistake."

The deputy points to Hunter's left arm. "It looks like you have a bandage under your shirt sleeve, what happened?"

"Burned it on the pizza oven at work."

"Oh you're not at the Green Iguana anymore?"

"No."

"You know the person who lit the fire that burned the sailboat probably has burns on his arm. The camera caught him running from the burning boat with the left arm of his sweatshirt on fire."

"Well, I burned my arm on the pizza oven."

The deputy, tired of playing games said, "Mr. Tyson, we have positively identified you at the marina near the boat when it caught fire. We have photographic evidence of you running from the fire with your left sleeve on fire. You have admitted you have burns on your left arm, now cut the crap and start cooperating. We know you did it, now why did you do it?"

Hunter stood silent for a while staring at the floor thinking of the evidence the deputy had against him and in his mind reviewing his options.

Hunter looked up at the deputy with an expression of defeat and says, "He got me fired from my job at the Green Iguana."

"Who did?"

"The guy with the sailboat. He and his drunken dancing girls held up traffic on US1 and I got fired."

IT'S AN INVASION

"Lookit, that place looks cute," Tom says, driving down US 1 pointing to the yellow and lime green building.

"Not cute," Linda corrected him, "Keyzie. That's what they call it down here. It looks Keyzie. Let's stop and have a drink."

"Naw, we're only 20 miles from Key West, let's keep going."

"Oh, come on. We have ten days to walk Duval Street with thousands of new friends, let's stop and see this place. I like the name, Mangrove Mama's. Very Keyzie."

Tom, a city boy born and raised in a Chicago suburb was not comfortable with what he called the jungle atmosphere of the Florida Keys. To him the whole string of islands looked like some old Tarzan movie. Reluctantly he pulled off the highway onto the crushed coral parking lot. Linda opened the door and jumped out eager for a new experience. Before opening the door Tom rolled down the window and looked at the ground, making sure there wasn't anything creeping, crawling or slithering.

"Come on ya big baby!" Linda called.

They walked into the front door and were welcomed with a very Keyzie decor; colorful lobster trap floats hanging from the ceiling, old fishing nets, mounted tuna, barracuda, and tarpon adorned the walls. A little out of character was a taxidermy full size standing black bear, a clawed paw raised the paw holding a beer mug, strings of plastic beads caught from a Key West Fantasy Fest parade float hung around the bear's neck and a tropical straw hat perched atop its head.

"I love it!" Linda said. Scanning the interior, taking it all in. "I love it!"

A pretty lady with long hair cascading off her shoulders offered the couple their choice of inside or outdoor seating.

"Let's go outside," Linda said. "Outside is good isn't it Tom? We're in the Keys we need to be outside."

Tom stepped to the door to the outside seating area, peeked out at the picnic tables and round tables under large colorful umbrellas surrounded by lush landscaping. "Are there any creatures out there?"

Linda looked disgusted, but the pretty hostess answered with a smile. "Just the occasional gecko. Nothing too scary."

Seated under a red and white umbrella, the hostess gave them menus and took their drink order, saying "Bonita, will be serving you today." They ordered drinks, a Key Lime Martini for Linda and an iced tea for Tom.

The only other person seated in the outdoor area was an elderly man sitting at a pink and purple painted picnic table. He sat with a clear view of the young couple smoking cigarettes and sipping a beer. Linda took noticed of the man. His face wore the lines of years of toiling in the sun, every wrinkle told a story, the chapters of his life. His white stubble of beard stood in contrast to his browned skin, the texture of his face was that of old leather from years of cigarette smoke. She noticed he wore a jacket in the heat of the Florida sun and long pants. A cap, faded and ragged from years of service covered his head. The slender man sat with one leg crossed over the other at the knee, he was hunched over a bit, she thought probably from a life of physical labor.

Tom, looking at the menu asked Linda what she was getting to eat.

"I'm not sure." They checked out the menu, Linda excited to be sitting outside eating while her friends back home were shoveling snow, ordered blackened mahi tacos. "I'm in the Keys and I'm gonna take in as much of the local life as I can. Tom, what are you getting?"

"I think I'd like the burger."

"Oh, come on Tom, we're in paradise, order something Keyzie. Try the lobster reuben or the mahi sandwich. Come on boy live on the edge."

"Nope, I want a burger."

"How about a tropical pizza?' Linda said reading from the menu. "They have one with andouille, shrimp, jambalaya sauce, bell pepper, onion, and pepperjack or we could split the Frutti De Mare. It has shrimp, bay scallops, mahi mahi, tomato sauce, fresh basil, caramelized onions, jalapeño and smoked mozzarella. What do you think Tom want to split a tropical pizza?"

"You have to be kidding, that sounds gross, I want a hamburger."

Tom refused cheese, lettuce, onion, tomato, ketchup, mustard and mayo. "Just the meat on a bun please. And well done, he told Bonita.

"At least get cheese, you know a cheeseburger in paradise."

"No, I want a plain hamburger."

The couple were a vision of contrast, she in a tied dyed tank top, white short shorts and flip flops he dressed in a button down shirt, jeans, white socks and Nike's.

Linda was on vacation, and she was going to enjoy herself in spite of her stick in the mud boyfriend. She was bouncing her head, tapping her toes and dancing in her seat to Howard Livingston and Mile Marker 24 band coming from speakers hidden in the landscaping. Sipping his tea, Tom sat with feet planted on the ground, his head down looking from side to side, sure something was going to sneak up and bite him.

Exhaling a blue cloud of smoke the old man asked, "What ya looking for son? Ya drop something?"

Tom looked at the man with an expression of, are you talking to me?

"Ya keep looking at the ground. What ya looking for?"

"Ah, nothing."

Linda spoke up, "He read an article that said there are pythons down here and he is sure one is going to sneak up on him."

The old man's twisted arthritic fingers stubbed out his cigarette in a nearly full ashtray, pushed his cap up and said. "Yeah, them pythons are in south Florida. A bunch of 'em. They are an invasive snake, ya know. People get 'em as pets and when they get too big to handle they let 'em go. A couple have been found up in Key Largo but they're mostly in the Everglades. They're eatin' up the small animals in the Glades, screwing up the ecological balance of nature. But, no need to worry about them down here. Not yet anyways."

Linda looked at the old man thinking he is probably not as old as he looks, he just didn't handle the test of time well.

Tom not quite convinced said, "They're hunting them too. I read about a state sanctioned hunt."

"Yeah, the State organizes hunts. On one they killed 80 of them snakes."

"Eighty, that's pretty good," Linda said.

The old man slowly, as if in pain, uncrossed his legs, grabbed the knee of his pants and lifted his other leg up onto the opposite knee.

"Eighty ain't much when you consider they think there could be a couple hundred thousand of them bastards in the Glades. But we got plenty of other invasive species down this way."

Tom was relieved to hear python were not an issue in the lower Keys but wasn't so happy to hear about other creatures.

"Like what?" Tom asked, lifting his feet to the rung of the chair looking around under the table.

The man put a cigarette between his lips, struck a match, cupped the flame with his hand, pursed his lips and blew out the flame with smoke. "Well, let's see," he said taking a long drag. "Well, there's you tourists invading our Keys and turning paradise into a trash heap, but there are the iguanas?"

Linda answered, "We saw one last night at the motel in Islamorada."

Tom added, "It scared the hell out of us."

"Yeah, they're everywhere down here. They ain't native. They come from South America, I think. But people get'em as pets and let them go. They like our climate and they keep popping out little lizards. Now there's so many of them they are a nuisance, eating people's flowers, shitting all over."

Tom looked in the manicured landscaping of Mangrove Mama's and asked, "Do they bite? I mean should we be afraid of them?"

"Naw, they are afraid of people. You get near 'em and they skedaddle. They just eat vegetation, not people."

"What other invasive species are there in the Keys?" Linda asked.

The old man coughed, clearing his throat with a hacking of a man with lung issues then said, "We got some plants that ain't from here originally and are choking out the native plants. The Beach Naupaka and Brazilian Pepper are a couple. They were imported cause people thought they was pretty now we can't get rid of 'em.

Tom asked, "What other invasive creatures should we be looking out for?"

"In the water we got Lionfish."

"Lionfish?" Tom asked surprised, wondering if the man was making it up.

"Yeah, it's a fish from the Pacific Ocean that people got for their aquariums and let go. They eat anything that moves, mate and have a lot of little Lionfish. There ain't nothing in these waters that will eat 'em so they just keep multiplying and killin smaller fish, wreckin' the ocean."

The waitress interrupted when she brought their meals. She asked the old man, "Zeke, are you bothering these nice folks?" She turned to Linda and Tom, "Just ignore him. He's an old coot."

"Oh, no," Linda said." He's been telling us about the invasive species that are in the Keys. It's interesting."

She turned to Zeke and asked, "Did you tell them about the monkeys?"

"Monkey's?" Tom asked. "There are monkeys in the Keys?"

"Oh yeah, use ta be thousands of 'em."

Tom was thinking that the old man was exaggerating although he did think the Keys resembled Tarzan's jungle. Tom asked, "I did a lot of research on the internet before we came down here and I didn't see anything about wild monkeys."

Stubbing the butt in the ashtray and shaking the pack for another, the man continued. "Back in 1973 a company brought in a bunch of monkeys. Eight hundred of em."

Bonita added, "It was the Linda les River Laboratories Company."

Zeke added, "Brought in the monkey's from India, Rhesus Monkeys."

Tom was afraid of snakes and lizards in the Keys, but he was skeptical about the monkey tale the old man was spinning. "Why would a company bring monkeys from India to the Keys?"

The waitress, with apparently nothing else to do sat down at the table with the old gentleman saying, "The company raised monkeys for medical research."

Tom shook his head in agreement thinking, "Okay, that sounds believable."

Zeke continued, "The company was from somewhere up north, I think one of them little New England states, bought a couple of islands,

Raccoon Key and Lois Key, and let the critters loose on 'em. It was cheaper to let the monkeys roam free on a island than build a building and a bunch of cages. The monkeys stayed on the islands cause they didn't like ta swim. It was a perfect deal for the company. All they had to do was take "Monkey Chow" and fresh water out to the islands a couple of times a week and the monkeys were happy and kept screwing till there was like 3,000 of 'em."

Bonita said, "My Grandpa worked with Zeke taking the chow out to the monkeys. He used to say they would screech and howl, jump around and carry on like crazy when they showed up."

"Yeah, them were noisy beasts alright. When the company got an order for some monkeys then we'd go to one of the islands and catch whatever the order said. Usually young ones but sometimes they wanted older males or females. Whatever they needed for the study they was doin'. But, ya had to be careful, them critters could scratch the hell out of ya." He said pulling up his sleeve displaying white scars the length of his wrinkled, skinny well-tanned forearm."

"They could make money raising monkeys?" Linda asked.

Zeke answered, "Hell yeah, anywheres from $1,500 to $4,500 apiece. The company was makin' good money."

"That much?" Linda said.

"The monkeys were especially desirable because they were free roaming, and didn't have a lot of the viruses and stuff monkeys from other grow sites did. The Key's monkeys were in demand," Bonita said.

Tom suspected they were pulling his leg. A monkey island in the Florida Keys sounded unbelievable. He thought, "I bet they pull this monkey crap on all the tourists."

Zeke continued his monkey tale, "It was going good. Locals and tourists used to go out to the monkey Keys in boats just to see the critters. When a boat got close the monkeys on the beach would raise holy hell. People loved 'em. But then a couple of 'em musta got off the island, and started hangin' out in the neighborhoods scaring people. The cops had ta shoot 'em."

Linda, was absorbed in the story, possibly because she was on her third Key Lime Martini and asked, "Are they still there? Can we go see them? I'd love to see them. Tom, can we rent some kayaks and go see them? Please Tom."

Without giving her request any thought he responded, "No."

Zeke said, "They ain't there no more anyway. The company had to take 'em off the islands in the 1990's cause of environmental reasons."

"Yeah, the monkeys ate the chow but they liked the leaves of the red mangrove trees for desert, Bonita said.

"So?" Linda said.

"Well, they ate all the leaves on the trees, killt the trees. When the trees died their roots couldn't keep the ocean from eroding the soil and the island was washing away. It became a real problem."

Taking a sip of the green concoction in the glass before her, Linda asked, "So what did they do?"

Bonita said, "The company tried to stop the monkeys from getting to the mangroves around the island. They put up electric fences but the monkeys just climbed over them or walked in the water to get around them.

Zeke said, "And, I don't think the company planned on the monkey population gettin so big. And when ya got thousands of monkeys, ya got a whole lot of monkey shit. When it rained the crap ran off the islands into the ocean. Polutin' the water with monkey poop."

Bonita, ignoring the hostess calling her, said, "Florida environmental protection got involved in the monkey business because the red mangroves are protected, and the critters were destroying them and the poop was polluting the ocean. They took the company to court and lawyers from both sides were fighting it out."

Zeke shook his head agreeing with Bonita and said, "The company agreed to get rid of the monkeys, restore the mangroves and clean up the poop. Then they would deed the two keys over to the state."

Bonita added, "Yeah, some said the company should have been held criminally responsible for what they did to the environment. The executives should have been sent to prison. Those keys are still a mess. They planted some mangroves on Raccoon and Lois Keys but it's nothing like it used to be."

"It'll take a couple decades, that's fer sure., Zeke said, lighting another cigarette and blowing a plume of smoke into the air.

Tom and Linda thanked Zeke and Bonita for the information, paid their tab and left a healthy tip. Back in the car Linda said, "Isn't it great we stopped and learned so much about the local history."

Tom looked at Linda saying, "I think that was a bunch of bullshit. I bet they are in their laughing their asses off at the way the two tourists fell for their monkey crap. It's probably a well-rehearsed con they pull on us northerners. I'm surprised they didn't want to sell us tickets for a boat to go out and see the monkeys."

Tom merged onto US 1 and joined the parade to Key West while Linda played with her phone. "Tom, it's not bullshit. I Googled it, it's all true. There were two islands down here for about 20 years that were populated with 3,000 Rhesus Monkeys. It is all true."

THINGS THAT GO BUMP IN THE NIGHT

"No, I'd better not," Sue said placing her hand over her glass. "I have to drive home. Oh, what the hell, just a half of a glass."

Karen's 50th birthday party was a success. Sue's BFF was surprised and happy to be remembered by her friends. Drinks flowed and gifts were opened, some of the funnier came from the Lovers Boutique.

Karen, a bit unsteady on her feet walked Sue to her car and hugged her best friend since she had moved to the Florida Keys. Sue steadied Karen, even though she wasn't so steady herself.

"Thank you so much for the party," Karen slurred and giving Sue a wet sloppy kiss on the lips. "Be careful driving home."

In her car Sue took a deep breath and held her hand over her mouth while she exhaled, smelling her breath. Before turning the key, she took a stick of Juicy Fruit from her purse. After chewing it a few times she put another stick in her mouth deciding two had to be better than one.

To get from Karen's to her house Sue would drive up the Overseas Highway for about 4 miles, then veer right onto County Road 905 through the Crocodile National Wildlife Refuge. There usually wasn't much traffic.

On 905 there weren't many street lights and the crescent moon was low in the sky, only occasionally visible between the palms like some ghostly aberration. The road was dark, her one operational headlight the only illumination. She drove slower than the limit, concentrating on keeping the car in her lane.

Her vision was blurry, the painted lines on the road sometimes wavered and sometime crossed, she learned from experience if she drove with one eye closed it helped.

"Stay awake!" she yelled at herself, opening the windows to let fresh air in and cranking up the air conditioner. It didn't help, she kept nodding off. When her right wheels drove off onto the gravel shoulder, she jerked awake from the alcohol induced slumber.

The road was so dark, so sparsely traveled and the area resembled a jungle, if she drove off the road she knew might not be found until the animals of the Crocodile National Wildlife Refuge ate her or she died of terminal mosquito bites.

She drove on, two hands in a death grip on the steering wheel. She forced herself to keep her heavy eyelids wide open fighting to stay awake. "Just a few more miles," she told herself.

Succumbing to sleep, she slipped to dreamland, until her car struck something. The front tires rode up over an object and the car bounced as the rear tires rode over it too.

"Oh my god! I hit something!" She slammed on the brakes, looked in the rear-view mirror then turned to look out the rear window. It was too dark.

"What did I hit?" She wondered. "Maybe I should get out and check." But the darkness changed her mind. "Should I call the police?" she asked herself, but she shouldn't be driving, and she couldn't afford another DUI.

"It was probably just a palm frond that fell onto the road," Sue tried to convince herself.

"I'd better get home," she said as she slid her Ford Fusion into drive and left the scene faster than she arrived.

The next morning, she awoke with an intense pain that started between her eyes and traveled to the top of her skull and down the back of her head to her spine. She laid on her bed, fully clothed, a waste basket of vomit at the side. She wondered what time it was but was afraid to open her eyes to check. It was morning she could tell by the sunshine pouring in through the window blinds.

She laid on top of the bedspread, trying to remember the night. Karen laughing and opening her gifts, the pitchers of Margaritas, the drive home. "Shit, the drive home!" she said aloud remembering. "I hit something on the way home."

"I wonder what it was, probably a raccoon there are a lot of them in the National Wildlife Refuge. I just hope it wasn't someone's dog. Please don't let it be someone's pet. I would feel terrible if it was someone's dog. But then in the Refuge there are all kinds of animals; woodrats, crocodiles, snakes, raccoons, alligators. It could have been anything," she said trying to convince herself.

"I should never have driven home. Why didn't someone at the party stop me, take my keys away."

The warmth of the shower felt good on her body. She leaned against the wall letting the water pelt her body soothing the throbbing in her head. With eyes closed, and the water massaging her, Sue drifted off to the memory of last night; she laughed remembering gag gifts Karen received, a bottle of Geritol, a package of Depends, a walker retrieved a dumpster, and the obligatory gift for a single woman, a giant vibrating dildo.

From the shower Sue could hear her cell ringing, rather playing, "All you need is love." She was so comfortable in the shower she was tempted to let it go to voicemail, but she was one who had a curious mind. Quickly drying off she ran to the bedroom. The phone had stopped ringing but the display read she had a missed call from Karen Johnson. She hit redial.

"Sue are you alright? Did you make it home okay?"

"Yeah, why?"

"I heard on the radio this morning that a guy was hit by a car last night on 905. I was worried you were in an accident."

Sue was quiet for a moment. "Ah, no, I'm okay. I didn't hit anything."

"Shit, was it a man I hit on 905?" She thought, but tried to appear to Karen like nothing had happened. The two exchanged memories of the birthday party and laughed at the giant vibrating rubber appendage. Sue was quick to get off, she had to think about what she might have hit last night. "Was it a man? Did I kill a man last night while I was so drunk?"

She quickly pulled on a tank top and shorts, not taking time for underwear, and ran out to check her car.

"No damage to the front end. Maybe I just imaged hitting something," she thought. Squatting down to get a good look she said, "Son of a bitch." There was a something in the front right wheel well. She touched it, it was blood. "Shit, I hit that guy last night. I killed a person while I was drunk!"

Sue's first instinct was to run. Pack up everything and run home, back to New Jersey. Her daddy would take care of her. He would know what to do. But, she also knew what he would say, "You did it, now go to the cops and tell them."

"I have to turn myself in. I was taught to the do the right thing. Now maybe some kids don't have a father because of me, or a woman doesn't have a husband." Before she changed her mind she dialed 911.

When the deputy knocked on her door she was a wreck, she had been crying and vomiting, her hair was a matted mess, her eyes were red and swollen, mascara running in rivers of tears.

The deputy took down all her information, took her statement, then went out to inspect the car. He took several photographs of the front, sides and wheel wells of the car. He took samples of the blood and placed the cotton swabs in plastic bags to be sent to the lab.

She asked, "Who did I hit? Are they okay?"

The deputy replied, "I'm sorry, I can't answer your questions, the case is under investigation."

He took a second tour of the car, making sure he hadn't missed anything, took a few more photographs. "Miss Gorman, you did the right thing to call this in. Do not leave the islands. A detective will be contacting you."

Throughout the morning Sue cried, paced, thought about the person she hit, wondered how badly injured they were or if they were dead. She was lighting her tenth cigarette of the day when her cell rang. With a shaking hand she picked it up and looked, it was an unknown caller.

"Hello?" She timidly said, afraid of what she was about to hear.

"Ms. Gorman?" a female voice said.

"Yes."

"This is Detective Shirk with the Monroe County Sheriff's Department. I was given your name and phone number by the deputy who took your report. First I want to thank you for taking responsibility for your actions and calling our office."

Sue, holding back tears asked, "Is the guy, okay? I mean is he alive?"

"Yeah, he is going to be laid up for a while, he has a broken hip, leg, wrist and a few ribs, but he'll live. He is out of surgery now and we got a chance to talk to him."

"All he is worried about is when he can get back out to the Glades and hunt again. He's an amateur python hunter. I need to ask you a few questions I was wondering if I could stop out at your place in about an hour?"

"Oh. The realization that they were coming to arrest her caused Sue to hesitate. "Ah, sure, I'll be here."

Questions flooded her mind; "What should I do? Should I call my dad? Should I call a lawyer? Who's going to water my plants?"

She emptied the vomit waste basket from her bedroom, sprayed air freshener hoping to mask the odor, and took another long shower, not knowing when she would have an opportunity to shower without guards watching.

Hair still damp, she sat on the couch, a brush in hand wondering what jail would be like. "Will I be in the county jail on Stock Island or in one of the State's prisons? Am I going to be abused by other inmates? I watched Orange is the New Black, am I going to become some woman's bitch?"

She had to stop asking herself the questions and get ready. She dried her hair and put on makeup so she would look good in her mugshot. She and her friends always check the Monroe County Sheriff's Office, M.C.S.O. arrests website and she wanted to look halfway decent in her booking photo. She changed her blouse three times and pants twice before she settled in her "going to jail" outfit, the last civilian clothes she would wear before putting on a prison jump suit. "I hope they aren't orange, orange isn't a good color for me, she thought.

Sue was sitting on the couch sipping a cup of coffee when she heard a car pull into her driveway, a quick peek through the blinds and she saw it was a Sheriff's patrol car. She had a sickening feeling in her stomach, she fought back the erg to vomit.

"Hello, Ms. Gorman? I'm Detective Shirk, we talked earlier."

"Come in," Sue said resigned to the fact that her next few years would be behind bars.

"Ms. Gorman, I have a few questions for you."

"Yes, whatever you want to know."

"About what time did you hit the bump in the road you described to the deputy who took the initial call?"

"Ah," Sue was thinking. Last night was kind of a fog to her. "I think it was around 11:00 or 12:00."

The detective wrote the answer in her notebook. "You said you felt your car hit something. Why didn't you stop?"

Her hands clenched in fists, she answered. "I did stop. I looked back and didn't see anything. It was dark. I figured it was probably a raccoon or a palm branch or something."

Detective Shirk wrote down her answer.

"When did you notice the blood on your car?"

"This morning. I wanted to check my car and make sure there wasn't any damage."

More writing. "Ms. Gorman, do you have any questions of me?"

"I feel so terrible about this; it was so dark I never saw him," Sue said tears welling up in her eyes.

The detective looked at her and asked, "Never saw who?"

The man I hit, I never saw him and when I looked back it was so dark I couldn't see him. I am so sorry."

Ms. Gorman, we tested the blood on your car and it came back conclusively to be from a Burmese Python. You ran over one of the python's that are overtaking the Everglades. It was a big one too, about 12 feet. You didn't hit the man."

"He was road hunting for the snakes. When he found the one you ran over and killed he got excited and jumped out of his truck and was stuffing it in a pillow case to turn it in for the bounty. But in his excitement he didn't take his truck out of gear and it rolled forward and ran him over. The guy got run over by his own truck."

The detective ripped a sheet of paper off her clipboard handing it to Sue and said, "Here this is an accident report for your insurance company in case you have any damage."

Sue took the paper, her mouth hanging open in disbelief. She thanked the detective and plopped down on the couch. She had mentally prepared herself to be arrested. She was ready for her mugshot; her hair was curled, her makeup was impeccable, she wore the outfit she thought would be her last before prison orange. She had envisioned her life behind bars, the abuse she would endure, the humiliation. "Oh, my God!" she exclaimed. "My guardian angel was working overtime."

Sue closed her eyes and said a prayer of thanks, swearing she would change her ways. She said aloud, "This is the day I quit drinking."

FRANK SINATRA IS MISSING!

"Have you seen Frank Sinatra lately?" Henley asked Austin.

"No, not in a day or two. Why?"

"Oh, nothing, he is usually by the pool, but I haven't seen him lately. Maybe he is off chasing one of the females. You know him."

"Austin if you see him let me know, the doctor will be here tomorrow and needs to see him."

Austin went to meet a group of people waiting at the front gate and Henley continued searching for Frank. She checked around the pool, in the main house, in the carriage house and walked through the gardens. No Frank.

"Dammit Frank, where are you hiding?"

"Marsha, have you seen Frank Sinatra lately?" Henley asked.

"Yesterday I saw Frank and John Wayne chasing Bette Davis behind the carriage house. But I haven't seen him today."

"I can't find him anywhere."

Marsha offered, "He probably snuck off, he is quite the tomcat, you know."

The following day at the morning staff meeting, the employees munched on donuts and sipped coffee. It was Johnny's turn to provide the morning treat and he liked donuts, not all that granola and bran muffins, healthy stuff, the others brought.

"I need everyone to be on the lookout for Frank Sinatra, he seems to have snuck off somewhere and Dr, Reyes is coming and needs to check the rash on his stomach. If it hasn't improved, we will have to apply an ointment to it daily."

"Oh, he won't like that," Marsha said.

"I know, it might take two of us to hold him down to rub it on."

Johnny wiped his shirt of powdered sugar which fell from his donut to his stomach and said, "I don't think Frank could have escaped the grounds, I watch the front gate pretty close, and he couldn't have gotten out without me seeing him."

Mel, the gardener, reported, "I found a hole dug under the fence in the backyard. You think Frank snuck off the grounds that way?"

Austin answered, "I highly doubt it, Frank isn't a digger."

Mel added, "Now Clark Gable likes to dig, I'm always filling holes from Clark."

Maria, the housekeeper, added, "I was all though the main house today and I didn't see Frank. But I did chase Joan Crawford and Humphrey Bogart off Mr. Hemingway's bed this morning."

"Hey Henley," Johnny interrupted, "You might want to ask Dr. Reyes to check out Charlie Chaplin. I saw him the other day and he was scratching his stomach. Maybe whatever Frank has is contagious."

"Good point, thanks Johnny. Okay everyone there are three cruise ships in today, and we'll be busy. And keep a watch out for Frank Sinatra and I guess Charlie Chaplin too."

Johnny sat in the little booth at the front gate selling tour tickets. On the steps of the Hemingway House, Austin stood before a group, some wearing cruise ship name tags and others were land bound visitors to Key West. He told them that Ernest and Pauline Hemingway purchased the Asa Tift house in 1931 and lived here until 1940 when Papa moved to Havana, Cuba.

"One day Mr. Hemingway was having a drink at Sloppy Joe's, not an unusual occurrence, and they were remodeling the bathroom. Much to Pauline's dismay he brought home one of the used urinals. It still sits where Mr. Hemingway left it," he said pointing to the cement and porcelain full length urinal lying on its back. "Now it's a watering trough for the 50 cats that roam the grounds of the Hemingway house."

Austin paused for a moment while the tourists took photographs. He took the opportunity to quickly text Henley.

"While living in Key West Mr. Hemingway was given a white kitten he named Snow White. The kitten was polydactyl, meaning that it had six toes rather than the normal five. All the cats you see on the grounds today are decedents of Snow White and have six toes. Mr. Hemingway always named his cats after famous people, for example over there by the red bougainvillea are John Wayne and Katherine Hepburn."

As Henley walked up, Austin pointed to the urinal telling the guests, "And there's Frank Sinatra taking a drink."

THE CONCH REPUBLIC REVOLUTION

A fictionalized account of a true event

In 1982, they gathered in a small house away from prying government eyes and ears. Curtains were drawn. Cigar and cigarette smoke hung over the participants in a blue haze. Beer bottles, both empty and full, a half dead whiskey bottle, several shot glasses and an overflowing ashtray filled the table. "We need to do something!"

"Yeah, the government border patrol check point is killing us. They are searching all the cars, looking for drugs and illegal immigrants. There are traffic backups for miles."

"Where is the check point exactly?" someone asked?

"It's on US 1 north of where County Road 905 meets US 1, sort of in front of the Last Chance Saloon. Ya can't get out of the Keys without them stopping and searching your car."

"I heard it was a nineteen mile back up on the 18 mile stretch for people going north," Fishbone added.

Ricky, with callused hands from working the shrimping fleet, gave his opinion, "I think we should get our guns and attack the check point, kill the mother fuckers. They can't shoot us all."

Sonny, said, "Simmer down, that ain't the way to do it. We gotta use our heads."

A bartender from Irish Kevin's said, "They're holding up traffic at the border just like between East and West Germany. I say it's time we revolt."

"Now hold on." Lindy, the only woman in the room who seemed to have the most common sense and was the soberest of the bunch said, "We should try to work within the system. We should appeal the government's decision to blockade the road and officially request them to cease and desist. Can we get a lawyer to draw up a letter to be delivered to the bureaucrats?"

"We already protested how we are being treated but all 'The Man' did was tighten its grip on us, put up a border crossing, they are holding us captive."

"Did you see the article in Life Magazine? It showed a lineup of cars trying to get through the check point. People going north were pissed, late for their airplanes, missing their Greyhound. The article made it look like you couldn't get out once you got in."

"Yeah, Mike at the Keys Hotel said people are canceling their reservations. People don't want to come if it takes hours to get out. And Jimmy said his sales are down 20% at the bar. This check point shit is hurting us in the pocketbook."

The woman added, "Not just the owners, but everybody. I had to lay off part of my housekeeping staff, so my girls don't have a check coming in to feed their families. And my boyfriend tends bar, and he had his hours cut cause there are less people coming to town because of the check point."

They all agreed that something had to be done.

The United States, in their war on the illegal smuggling of drugs and Cuban, South American and Haitian immigrants into the Florida Keys built a check point on US 1 to curb the flow of contraband from leaving the Florida Keys.

From mainland Florida there are only two roads leading to the string of islands; the causeway to Key Largo, called the 18-mile stretch and County Road 905 named Card Sound Road. The U.S. Border Patrol built a check point just beyond where the two roads merge so no matter which route you took out of the Keys you had to pass through the roadblock.

Dennis Wardlow, the mayor of Key West, and the city council made a formal complaint to the federal government protesting the Border Patrol actions, citing its negative impact on tourism in Key West and throughout the entire string of islands.

Not receiving any relief, the mayor and council filed an injunction in a federal court asking the government to stop the check point on economic grounds. The court sided with the Border Patrol and the check point remained.

As tourists changed their plans and went to other sunny locations where they wouldn't have to sit for hours at a road block as they tried to return home, fewer people walked Duval Street, fewer shopped, ate or drank, and more and more people were laid off.

At the April 23, 1982, city council meeting a large group of angry constituents voiced their frustrations, prompting the mayor and council to make a decision to take action. They declared that since the United States established a border check point and was treating them like a separate country, they would secede from the United States and form their own nation, The Conch Republic.

A person who was born and raised in the Keys is a called a Conch, thus the new republic was called the Conch Republic. The new republic took the motto, "A sovereign State of Mind." Peter Anderson, Secretary General of the republic announced The Conch Republic's goal was to seek to bring Humor, Warmth and Respect to a world in need of all three.

Mayor Wardlow was proclaimed to be the Prime Minister and his first order of business was to declare war on the United States! He broke a loaf of Cuban bread and struck a man dressed in a United States Navy uniform as an act of war then quickly surrendered to the man. As any nation would do at the end of a war, the Conch Republic applied to the United States for one billion dollars in foreign aid.

The new nation declared their own currency, the sand dollar, issued passports and an official flag.

The stunt succeeded in bringing the plight of the Florida Keys to the rest of the nation. Magazines covered the secession of the island and it was featured in newspapers across the county, resulting in an embarrassment for the federal government. The border patrol check point was soon removed, but the Conch Republic remained.

In 1995, the United States Army Reserve organized a training exercise of an island invasion. They planned on landing on a beach in Key West, unfortunately the Army failed to notify the City of Key West of the plan. Seizing on the opportunity to bring publicity to the island, the leaders of the 1982 secession retaliated to the Army's attack by boarding the schooner Western Union to attack a Coast Guard boat coming into port. The battle was short lived, the Conch Republic Navy attacked the boat with water balloons and the Coast Guard answered the marauders with their fire hoses. The Conch Republic quickly surrendered to live to fight another day.

The soul of the Conch Republic lives on to this day. And Key West still lives in a Sovereign State of Mind, bringing Humor, Warmth and Respect to a world in need of all three.

THE MISSILE SILO

The Monroe County Sheriff's Deputy Radak knocked on 323 C at the Ocean Surf Condominium complex in Tavernier, Florida. When he answered the door, Brendan McIntosh stared at the officer, afraid of what he might hear.

Trained in situational awareness and to be ever vigilant, the deputy's eyes automatically went to the glint of silver in McIntosh's right hand. However it wasn't a weapon; it was a 30 oz Yeti tumbler.

"Mr. McIntosh?"

"Yes."

"You filed a missing person's report for your roommate, a Jeremy Comings did you not?"

"Yes, last week. We had a disagreement and he stormed out. He has done it before when he doesn't get his way, but he always comes back in a day or two. This time he was gone five days, I got worried," Brendan said nervously.

"I'm afraid Mr. Comings was found deceased."

"What? Where? I mean what happened?"

The deputy pulled a notebook from his breast pocket and read, "The deceased was found in the Crocodile Lake National Wildlife Refuge. It appears he was killed by a python."

"Oh my god, oh my god. He's dead. A snake killed him? How do you know?"

"The medical examiner will make the final determination but a preliminary examination of bruising of his torso indicates a snake wrapped around his body and squeezed him to death."

"Where is he? When can I see him?" an obviously distraught Brendan asked.

"The body was taken to the county coroner's office. Are you named as his emergency contact?"

"Yes, of course."

"Then you will be notified when the body is to be released, and you can make arrangements. Can you tell me why he was at the Crocodile Lake National Wildlife Refuge?"

"He likes," Brendan paused to wipe away a tear and changed his statement to the past tense, "He liked to hike in the refuge. He especially liked exploring the old missile base."

The deputy, an amateur military history buff himself, was very familiar with the history of the area.

The Castro brothers, Fidel and Raul, overthrew the government of Fulgencio Batista, Cuba's President in 1959. Fidel Castro was named the new president and evicted all US investors and appropriated their land, factories, homes and businesses. In 1961, the CIA sponsored a group of 1,400 Cuban rebels to overthrow Castro and his communistic ideals. Castro's Cuban Revolutionary Armed Forces easily defeated the invading forces in three days. The failed attack became known as the Bay of Pigs Invasion after the location where attempted invasion occurred.

After the 1961 invasion attempt, the relationship between Castro and the Soviet Union grew. A year later a US high altitude surveillance U-2 spy plane provided photographic evidence of soviet medium-range missiles deployed in Cuba, less than one hundred miles from the United States. The US military established a naval blockade to prevent Soviet ships from delivering any more weapons to Cuba which led to what became known as the Cuban Missile Crisis of 1962.

United States President Kennedy and the Soviet President Khrushchev faced off for several tense days before it was agreed the Soviets would remove their missiles from Cuba in exchange for the US agreeing not to attempt to invade Cuba again and other concessions. Many historic and military scholars agree that this was the closest the world ever came to a nuclear war.

The United States military took steps to fortify our southern border by developing Nike-Hercules missile defensive firing positions around Miami and the Homestead Air Force Base on the mainland of the Florida peninsula. They also established missile launch sites in Key West and north Key Largo, positions within easy range of Cuba. The cold war between the Soviet Union and the United States continued for many years but weaponry technology advances made the missiles in the Keys obsolete, and the missiles in Key West were removed and the Key Largo site was shuttered.

The Deputy knew the Key Largo site had been abandoned for almost 60 years. The once crucial base; the launching area and Integrated Fire Control sites had been reclaimed by nature; trees and vines have overtaken The concrete radar mounts and other concrete structures, now part of Crocodile Lake National Wildlife Refuge, are still visible from County Road 905. The area is technically off limits to park visitors, but the abandoned missile base is a favorite with history and military enthusiasts.

Unfortunately, since the late 1990's, south Florida has been plagued by a population of Burmese pythons. Pet snakes were released in the Everglades by owners when they grew too difficult to care for, and others were accidentally released from a snake farm during a hurricane. The snakes flourished in the warm moist climate of south Florida and established a breeding population. Some snakes found their way to the Crocodile Lake National Wildlife Refuge in North Key Largo and were living in the area of the abandoned missile base.

Brendan told the deputy, "Jeremy loved exploring the cold war ruins and claimed no silly snakes would keep him from it. I guess this time a snake found him."

Four days later Brendan answered the knock at his door. Through the peephole he saw the same deputy who delivered the bad news about Jeremy and another deputy.

"Mr. McIntosh, you are under arrest for the murder of Jeremy Comings."

"What?"

"Turn around sir."

"Wait, what are you saying? What are you doing?" Brendan said, turning around, his hands pulled behind his back and handcuffs snapped in place.

"I didn't kill Jeremy. You yourself said a snake killed him. You said the pattern of bruises on his torso looked like a snake squeezed him to death."

The deputy turned Brendan until he was facing him, "You're right, Mr. McIntosh, Mr. Comings body showed signs of bruising as if a python wrapped around his body and squeezed. There were bruises on his neck and chest, and he had broken ribs indicative of a python attack. But the forensic team found the bruises were not from a python, rather they matched bruise pattern produced by a 30-ounce Yeti tumbler pressed into his body. A 30-ounce Yeti like you were carrying when I first came here. In fact, postmortem vividly revealed the distinct impression of the letter "Y."

"But, but..." Brendan stammered as he tried to think of what next to say. "But you said Jeremy died of suffocation. A Python kills by suffocating its prey."

"Mr. McIntosh it was thought that Python's killed by suffocation until 2015, when herpetologists discovered the Python kills by squeezing their prey until the heart can no longer pump blood through the body and the victim dies of a heart attack."

"Well, then Jeremy must have died of a heart attack when the snake had him in its grasp," Brendan said.

The deputy slowly shook his head in the negative. "No, Mr. McIntosh, Jeremy most definitely died of suffocation. The forensic investigator found bruising around his mouth and nose and when you applied pressure to whatever you used to suffocate Jeremy his teeth left an impression on the flesh inside his mouth."

Looking around the apartment the deputy said, "We will check those pillows on the couch. If they were used to kill Mr. Comings, they will carry residue of his saliva proving he died here in this room."

"But that doesn't prove I killed him," Brendan protested.

"Mr. McIntosh you told me you and Mr. Comings had a disagreement before he left the apartment. Your next-door neighbor collaborates with that statement. He told us the fight was far from a disagreement, what he heard was a violent struggle, with what sounded like a table being broken. Mr. McIntosh, where is your coffee table?"

"We never had one. I don't like tables in front of the couch, people put their feet on them, and they just collect stuff."

The deputy walked to the couch bent down to see the impression of four feet in the carpet. He looked up at Brendan, "I get the impression you're lying."

THE MUDDY RIVER TAVERN DUVAL STREET BAR CRAWL

Sitting around their regular table at the Muddy River Tavern, the four couples from Minooka, Illinois met each Thursday evening. One night the conversation revolved around taking a trip to Key West and doing the Duval Street Bar Crawl. It started out as just casual conversation, then a full-fledged competition of who could last the longest on a Duval Street Bar Crawl. There wouldn't be any cash prizes, just an old bowling trophy Tom would adapt for the occasion.

Once it was decided they would travel to Key West to challenge the notorious Atlantic Ocean to the Gulf of Mexico Duval Street, they discussed it every Thursday. After several suggestions they came up with a name: "The Muddy River Tavern Duval Street Bar Crawl", the TMRTDSBC. They had tee shirts made up with the name printed in black letters outlined in white on blue, yellow, red and orange tie-dyed shirts.

Karen suggested they should determine which bars to hit on what had taken on the abbreviated name "*The Crawl*."

Linda offered that they should start at Captain Tony's. Some argued that this was a Duval Street bar crawl and Captain Tony's wasn't on

Duval, it was on Green Street a half of block off Duval, so it shouldn't be included. But, Mell explained, "In the historical perspective of drinking in Key West, Sloppy Joe's saloon is the Mecca of tropical consumption." Those who had been to the southernmost city shook their heads in agreement, Mell continued, "The original location of Sloppy Joe's, Ernest Hemingway's favorite watering hole I might add, was originally where Captain Tony's is now. So, I think to show homage to Papa Hemingway and the tradition of drinking in Key West I think we need to include Captain Tony's."

Tom raised his glass and proposed a toast, "To Hemingway and wherever the hell he drank!"

It was decided the first drink would be at Captain Tony's.

"When?" Debby asked. "What time do we start?"

Wayne suggested, "We need to start early, ya know what they say, you can't drink all day if you don't start in the morning."

Karen asked, "Eleven? Or earlier?"

It was decided and Karen wrote in a Muddy River Tavern Duval Street Bar Crawl notebook, *The Crawl* will begin at 10:00 AM. The justification for the early start was so they could take a lunch break around noon.

Lynn said, "Alright, now that we have a name, a starting time and starting location, we need some rules."

Tom asked, "Rules, what rules? You lift a glass to your lips, you pour it in, and you swallow. Lift, pour, swallow. Lift, pour, swallow. We don't need no stinkin' rules."

Lynn continued, "For example, what will we be drinking? Mell always drinks rum and Coke, Jeff's preference is a bottle of Bud Light, Debby and I are winos, Wayne only drinks craft beer, preferably an IPA. Linda is a whiskey girl, Karen only consumes Dr. Pepper and Tom will drink anything, we need work out what to drink."

It was decided and Karen wrote in the notebook; At the first stop all contestants must drink a 12 once Bud Light. A shot of whiskey will be consumed at Sloppy Joe's, the second stop. At the legendary Hog's Breath Saloon each of the contestants will have a rum and Coke, their choice of diet or regular.

The group spent entirely too much time debating whether it should be rum and Pepsi or if it had to be Coke. After an hour they realized it didn't really matter.

The crew would next proceed to Irish Kevin's where they would eat lunch. The dining selection was up to the individual, but they had to drink a Blood Orange Sunset IPA, with a 6.7 ABV. Wayne said, "On top of all the other drinks it should be a real kick in the ass."

Linda asked, "What about the Flying Monkeys? We gotta go to the Flying Moneys, they have great frozen Margaritas."

Karen wrote it down saying, "I'm not sure of what order it will be in but, we'll include it."

Mell says, "We gotta include a stop at The Rum Bar, it's on Duval Street."

Jeff asks, "What's good there?"

"My favorite is the Pain Killer. It's rum, coconut cream and pineapple with a rum floater. It's delicious," Mell claimed.

Debby said, "I bet that'll thin the herd."

Linda asked, "What about the 801 Bourbon Bar?"

Mell playfully asks, "What's their specialty?"

Linda responds, "Ah duh, bourbon."

It was added to the list.

"That is probably enough, I doubt anyone will make it through that many drinks without vomiting," Karen said.

"And remember, ya puke and yer out," Wayne clarified.

Karen says, "But wait, we haven't included the Green Parrot yet."

"Or the Smallest Bar in Key West is really cute too," added Debby.

Tom, not always the voice of common sense spoke up surprising everyone. "I think we have enough. Let's save those for the second annual crawl."

Airfare from Chicago to Miami was purchased, a minivan rented and accommodations at the Conch Shell Inn were made. Karen, the designated driver during *The Crawl*, the designated lead walker, contacted each bar, explained what they were doing and got the price of the drinks. She tabulated the cost and collected the amount from each participant. They were ready for the first annual Muddy River Tavern Duval Street Bar Crawl"

As they boarded the aircraft, Wayne observed that it was only appropriate since they were going to Key West to indulge in spirits that they were flying Spirit Air. Linda and Tom shared a three-seat row with a man from Chicago in the window seat. Debby and Mell sat in the middle row with Jeff and Lynn and across the aisle were Karen and Wayne sharing a row with a nice Canadian woman going on holiday.

The flight went well, no turbulence, on time, a fun time for all. The only drawback was the sneezing kid seated behind Jeff who repeatedly kicked his chair and his little sister who noisily sucked snot back in her constantly dripping nose.

Their minivan was waiting in Miami and soon they were crossing the 18 mile stretch to the Keys. The sun was shining, the sky was blue, and the water looked inviting. The 100-mile drive to Key West was slow with bumper to bumper traffic allowing them to enjoy the view of the beautiful blue waters of the Gulf of Mexico and the Atlantic Ocean.

The next morning Tom asked Linda, "Are you ready for this?" as they dressed in their motel room at the Conch Shell Inn.

"I hope so. We've been preparing for it for weeks. The bigger question is, Tom, are you up to this. You're kinda a wimp."

"Hey, I can out drink you anytime."

"Well, let's go down pool side for the complimentary breakfast and prepare our stomachs," Tom said.

As they gathered for breakfast in the lush gardens by the pool, Debby told the group, "I read that we need to drink a glass of milk before drinking, it's supposed to be one of the best things to have before drinking alcohol."

"I thought it was water we were supposed to drink before drinking. It dilutes the alcohol in your system," Wayne volunteered.

"I don't know. I saw once that you should eat a lot of fruit. The fruit is rich in vitamins and minerals and is high in potassium, it will keep your body in balance. It reduces nausea when drinking," Linda interjected.

Tom added, "I think I read once in college during my heavy-duty drinking days that you should eat fruit with a high-water content, like watermelon, melon, and papaya. I hope they have that on the breakfast menu."

Wayne walked to the table with a tray filled with two plates of fruit, two glasses of water, two cartons of white milk and one black and one sugar and cream coffee for he and Karen.

"What the hell is that? You should be eating a big helping of pancakes, it'll stretch your stomach and allow you to drink more," Mell said, stuffing a forkful of syrup dripping pancake in his mouth.

Wayne replied, "My stomach is stretched out enough from last night's sloppy joe at Sloppy Joes."

Taking a sip of her Coke Linda said, "If you want to be able to hold your drinks you have to load up on sugar. I heard it helps breakdown the alcohol carbs in your system."

"I thought it was pickles you should eat before drinking," Karen said. "They have electrolytes and are salty."

Mell said, "I think you eat pickles before drinking to avoid a hangover."

"I guess we all have a different theory on what we need to do to consume a lot," Debby said.

Wayne wiped his mouth with the back of his hand and asked, "Mell, did ya bring the tee shirts"

"Yep, got 'em in my room. Debby pinned a note with names on them, so you get the right sizes ya all ordered."

Karen got up to take a commemorative photograph of the group and noticed, "Hey, where's Jeff?

Lynn rolled her eyes, "He's still in bed. His allergies are driving him nuts. I swear he was up half the night blowing his nose. He went through the box of tissue and started on the toilet paper. But he said he would be ready for *The Crawl.*"

Back in the room Mell was in the bathroom. Debby yelled, "Hey Mell, are you okay? You've been in there a while."

Mell exited the bathroom closing the door behind him saying, "I wouldn't go in there if I was you. My stomach is all out of whack. Do we have any Tums or Pepto-Bismol?"

Debby met up with Karen on her way to the front desk to see if they had any antacids. "Mell is sick. His stomach is rumbling, and he spent a lot of time on the toilet. I hope he is okay for the crawl."

Karen told Debby, "I heard Lynn went back to her room and brought her breakfast back up. She won't be doing the crawl."

Debby responded, "And I heard your allergies had you up all night."

Wiping her nose with a pad of toilet paper, Karen said, "Maybe it's not allergies, maybe it's those snot nose kids from the airplane. I bet they infected us."

Then Karen remembered Tom saying the guy next to him on the fight, slept all the way and he was, clammy and pale as a ghost. I wonder if we caught something from him?"

The contestants of The Muddy River Tavern Duval Street Bar Crawl, now The Muddy River Tavern Bathroom Stall Crawl, one by one came down with the illness. Some stayed in their room close to the bathroom, some went to sit around the pool hoping the sun would bake the germs from their bodies. All except Tom who seemed to have escaped the scourge.

Since The Crawl was canceled Tom took a walk down Duval for his own mini crawl. He thought he would celebrate his immune system, toast his good health, rinse his system with an alcohol bath.

When Tom got back to the Conch Shell Inn he found most of the gang at the pool, no one drinking a cocktail. Juice seemed to be the drink of the day.

Linda said, "Tom, you are so lucky you didn't get what we have. It is the worst. Jeff is still sick, squirting out both ends. Karen has been in bed all day and Debby couldn't make it back to her room and vomited in the landscaping."

Linda shaking her head sadly added, "The Hydrangea's will never be the same."

Tom, admitted, "Well, apparently, I didn't escape it. I puked today in town."

"Oh no," Mel said. "Are you alright? Where?"

"Well, let's just say I'm not welcome at Sloppy Joe's anymore."

THE HELICOPTER RIDE

On their way to Key West for a day of walking Duval, eating at Schooners Wharf and listening to Michael McCloud sing, people watching, and trying to drink the island dry, Jeremy said, "Every time we drive through Marathon, I see that Lime green helicopter at the airport taking people up on tours of the Keys. Ya know Laci, some time we should take the tour."

"...happy birthday dear Jeremy, happy birthday to you." Laci and the gang sang their off-key rendition to Jeremy. He bowed to the crowd accepting their celebratory lyrics honoring his forty-fifth trip around the sun.

Jeff held his glass aloft in a toast saying, "To Jeremy! May you be in heaven ten minutes before the devil knows you're dead."

Laci hugged Jeremy saying, "Open my gift, open it first." He took the envelope from her. With a rip to the end, he fished the letter out and read. He read it to himself remembering on his thirty-fifth birthday she gave him a packet of coupons redeemable for various sexual favors.

"Wow! Laci, this is great!"

Shouts of, "What is it?" came from the crowd.

"What did she give you this time?" Jen, Laci's best friend who helped create the coupons last time, asked.

"It's a gift certificate for a helicopter ride. Something I've always wanted to do."

After they showered and toweled each other dry Jeremy said, "This is the big day, our helicopter ride. I checked The Weather Channel, and it should be a sunny clear day. Only a 15% chance of rain in Marathon."

Driving south along US1, they stopped at Starbucks for some caramel coffee concoction for her and a plain old large black coffee for him. The sun was rising in a cloudless sky and not so much as a breeze moved the palms.

It was fifty miles from their Key Largo home to the Florida Keys/Marathon International Airport. Fifty miles of sunny sky, views of the Atlantic Ocean out the left window and the Gulf of Mexico out the right. They truly did live in paradise.

Walking into the general aviation building Jeremy told the lady behind the counter they were here for a helicopter ride. Her phone rang and she pointed to a desk. He and Laci walked to the desk where they were greeted, "Hi, are you my 11:00?"

"We are indeed," Jeremy said all smiles in anticipation of the adventure.

"I'm Ryan, your pilot today. Have you ever flown in a helicopter?"

Laci responded, "Nope, it's a first for both of us."

"Me too," Ryan said, quickly followed by, "Just kidding. I've been flying for 12 years. I just need you to sign these forms, then we'll be off."

Walking to the helicopter inside the gated secured enclosure, Ryan said, "You have selected the Sombrero Lighthouse and Seven Mile Bridge tour. It's a nice sunny day so we should be able to see all kinds of stuff."

"Like what?" Jeremy asked.

"Well, we often see Spotted Eagle Rays, sharks and sometimes turtles."

Laci climbed in the back of the four-person aircraft. Ryan showed her how to buckle the shoulder/lap harness, helped her with the headset and showed her how to open and secure the door. Then he showed Jeremy, sitting in the front seat, left of the pilot. Ryan took a walk around the lime green machine emblazoned with orange lettering outlined in white stating "Helicopter Tours!" The pilot did his preflight inspection of the aircraft surfaces and movable parts.

Climbing in his seat and strapping in Ryan said, "There isn't any air conditioning in this bird so leave the doors open until I tell you to close and secure them. It'll cool off once were airborne."

A flip of some toggles, a turn of a key and a push of a button and the rotors above slowly begin to spin, increasing speed with each rotation.

The pilot said something in his microphone to the tower and we slowly, almost hesitantly, lifted off the ground by a foot and a half and hovered as the pilot checked instruments and controls. More talk with the control tower and the helicopter rose, leaned forward and flew north climbing above the runway, leaving gravity to the earth bound.

"Oh my god, I love this!" Laci said in the microphone connected to her headset, holding her cell phone in photo mode to the window.

Jeremy nodded in agreement, his headset nearly sipping off. "This is fantastic." I feel like T.C. on Magnum.

From a 300-foot elevation the Atlantic stretched out before them in multiple hues of blue; darker where the water was deeper, a blue green where the bottom was covered with sea grass, and a beautiful turquoise blue where the bottom was sandy.

As they approached the Sombrero Lighthouse Ryan explained over the headsets, "The lighthouse was built in 1858 on Sombrero reef after several ships met their demise on the shallow reef. It is built of steel and wrought iron. The light was automated in 1960 and deactivated in 2015."

Ryan banked and circled the lighthouse. A dozen boats were moored at the anchorage with red and white dive flags flying while snorkelers swam, looking at the fish but secretly hoping to find a silver coin or two left from a wreck.

Ryan came over the headset to explain their next maneuver. "See that darker area ahead? It's a patch of sea grass. Watch for sharks where the blue of the sandy bottom meets the darker bottom. I'll descend a bit so you can see better."

Jeremy was leaning forward scanning the ocean looking for the black silhouette of a shark prowling the periphery of the sea grass, searching for lunch.

Laci looked out her side window, phone in hand ready to capture the creature. She said in her microphone, "Ah, I think I saw something."

Jeremy said, "What?"

Ryan asked, "What was it? A ray, a shark?"

Laci responded, "No. I know you're not going to believe this, but it looked like a skeleton."

"It was probably some coral that looked like a skeleton." Jermey said.

Laci was quick to defend her sighting, "No, I saw the white bones laying on the dark grass. It was a skeleton."

Ryan worked the controls, and the helicopter went into a slow dive and banked to the left above the sea grass.

"There!" Laci yelled. "Over there," She said pointing out her window.

The pilot banked right. "Heck, that sure looks like bones."

He maneuvered until the skeleton was just out his side window and hovered. "I don't know what it is. Could be a skeleton." He descended closer to the surface and grabbed his cell phone from his pocket.

A woman answered his call, "911, what is your emergence?"

Ryan explained what they had found, providing the longitude and latitude of the sighting.

"We've alerted FWC, Monroe County Sheriff's Office and the Coast Guard. Someone should be there shortly. They have requested that you remain on the scene until they arrive. It would make locating the object easier."

"Affirmative," Ryan answered.

While they hovered above the bones waiting for the emergency vessels to arrive, Laci was taking photographs of the bones hoping to get a good one for her Facebook page. Ryan explained, "I called 911 rather than call it in to Marathon tower over the radio because it is private. We don't need a bunch of curious boaters hearing a radio call and coming here looking for the skeleton."

Jeremy pointed and over his microphone said, "Look!" An orange Coast Guard boat was flying across the water with blue lights flashing.

"Coast Guard, this is helicopter N298BL. I am hovering over the item in question."

"Roger, N298BL. We have a visual on you."

The Coast Guard came to a stop under the helicopter, two divers quickly rolled over the starboard hull. From a height of 200 feet, Laci, Jeremy and Ryan had a front row seat in the action playing out below them.

They watched as a Coast Guard diver brought up a cement block with a rope attached to it. Laci, was the first to verbalize what the others were thinking. "Is this like a mafia hit or something?"

The second diver came to the surface and handed the skull up to the boat then went down for the remaining bones.

When he resurfaced, he tossed several bones up to the boat. The second diver did so also.

"Hello, N298BL. This is Coast Guard, 17313. We have retrieved the skeleton. It was anchored down by a cement block and broke up when we moved it. Thank you for your assistance."

"You're welcome Coast Guard 17313. The guy must have been down there for a while, looks like the bones were picked clean."

"Yeah, all that remained on the thigh bone was a price tag from Walmart."

Ryan asked astonished, "A price tag?"

The Coast Guard responded, "Yeah, it was a plastic Halloween decoration. Someone's idea of a prank."

BIG PINE KEY, MORE
THAN LITTLE DEER

"Dad we really need to clean out that old shed. There might be some good stuff in there, ya know some antiques you can sell."

"Which shed?"

"The one almost falling down east of the old milking parlor."

"Yeah, there is some old shit in that one. I ain't been in it for 10 years, oh hell probably 20 years or more. It's just a bunch of junk left over from my ma and pa, ya know your grandma and pappy. Let's see", he says, right hand scratching his chin. "I'm 79..."

"Dad, your 81."

"Oh yeah, I'm 81. Pa died when I was in my teens, 17 I think. He was changing a tire on the tractor, and it fell off the jack on him. We didn't know the tractor fell, Ma was cooking and I was on a date, with Cora Elyse Norwiski, I think, or maybe it was Audrey Pawloski, hell coulda been that Khloe Elizabeth or Ariel Louise girl, they was all sweet on me and I was dating 'em all.

An there Pa was, laying on the dirt floor of the machine shed, a tractor on his leg, crushed it good too. All bloody and bones sticking out. Really nasty. Doc Main said he woulda lived, if we found him right away, but we just thought he was working on the tractor, so we didn't go out to the shed to check on him. So, he sat on the ground with a tractor on his leg till his heart pumped all the blood outa his body."

"Dad, I know how Grandpa died, we were talking about the old shed and the stuff in it."

"Oh yeah. Anyway, Ma caught the cancer and died in 1971, or 1972 and I got the farm. I was sleepin' in the small bedroom upstairs and in the winter the heat from the wood stove didn't make it up there so good, it was cold."

"Dad, what's this have to do with the shed?"

"I'm getting there, Sweetie. Just hold yer horses."

"Anyway, when Ma died I moved ta the bedroom my folks useta use. Ya know one time it was so cold in my bedroom upstairs, a glass of water next to my bed froze. Yeah, frozen solid. You know what these winters are like."

"What about the stuff in the shed?"

"Well, I moved into Ma's bedroom. Slept in her bed, the one she died in, ya know. First it was kinda creepy an all, cause she died in the bed, same sheets and all, but I got used to it. It's not that she was gonna haunt me or nothing. I changed things some, moved the bed to the south wall cause it was next to the window and it was drafty. No matter what I did to that window, on a windy day the outside always got inside. I mean in the wither the wind was a blowin' an the curtain was movin'."

"Dad, the shed?"

"Yeah. I cleaned out Ma's closet and took her stuff to the shed. Ya know she had Pa's old navy uniform hangin' in the closet. Did you know that Pa was in the navy back in the 30's? He was ina submarine. Useta go all around under the water. That's not for me, nope, no way! I want ta be on the water not under the water."

"So it's a bunch of Grandma's stuff in the shed?"

"Yeah, and your grandpappy's too, probably."

"Dad, did you look in the boxes before you moved them?"

"I don't know, maybe. Maybe not. That was a long time ago. Don't know if there's any of that antique stuff in there, but it's a bunch of old shit, that's fer sure."

"Do you mind if I take a look in the shed?"

"Sure, go ahead. Take anything ya want. Jus careful in that shed, don't want the roof fallin' in on ya. Its fallin' down ya know."

"Hey, Becca, what are you doing?" Griffin asked finding his wife sitting on the living room floor with old cardboard boxes strewn about.

"I picked up some stuff at my dad's. These are boxes of my grandma's stuff from when she was young. I never knew her, she died long before I was born. Looking through her stuff is like I'm getting to know my grandmother.

I mean there are some old pictures of granny and pappa's from when they were young, they were on a beach and there are palm trees in the background."

"Can you tear yourself away from granny for dinner. I brought home Chinese. But wash up, your hands are filthy."

Getting up from the floor and looking at her hands, they were smudged with black. "The boxes are grimy, they've been stored in a shed for decades."

"Hey Bec, are you coming to bed?"

"In a little bit, Grif. I found some of granny's and pappa's letters from when they were dating. You should read these; they were so in love."

Reading one of the yellowed pieces of paper Becca said, "Grandpa must have written this while he was out at sea. He wrote that he misses grandma dearly and can't wait to get back to shore to be with her. He asks if she can get away from work when he gets back to spend some time with him. Then he bugs her about leaving her job and finding something else to do."

"Grif, I know neither grandma or grandpa went very far in school, maybe like fifth grade and their spelling and grammar show it. But I think its sweet that they still wrote each other."

"Or," Grif said, "They had someone else write the letters, someone who could read and write."

"Anyway, they did it, they found a way to stay connected when they were apart."

"So, tell me again why we are driving over 1,600 miles to the Florida Keys?" Grif asked Becca.

"My grandma and pappa met in the Keys when pappa was in the Navy stationed at the submarine base in Key West and granny was working down there."

"Do you know where she was working?"

"No, not really. She never said in her letters but wherever it was pappa didn't like it and would write telling her to quit and find another job."

"I wonder what she was doing?" Grif said.

Becca stared out the windshield as they drove down the 18 mile stretch into the Keys responded, "I don't know, farmwork; picking coconuts or pineapples or maybe she worked at a fish house, they can be dangerous places to work. I guess we will have to wait and see. I have the address where she lived from the letters."

"Are you sure it's down here?" Grif asked as they crossed another bridge. "We turned off US 1 a way back."

"Look! There's one of those Key Deer I read about. It's so cute. It's about the size of a dog. I could just cuddle it. Slow down, I want to get a picture."

"According to the GPS it should be around here somewhere."

"Is that it?" Becca asked.

"That's what the GPS says. 30813 Watson, Big Pine Key Florida," Grif answered slowing the car.

"Are you sure, it's a restaurant."

"Yeah, and a busy one from the looks of the people waiting outside."

Finding a parking spot was no easy task at this off-the-beaten path pub. Becca sat on one of the picnic tables where guests waited for a seat in the restaurant. Grif ordered a couple of "No Name Pub" beers and they sipped the cool beer enjoying the warmth of the sun waiting for a table to open inside.

"I know this is the address where pappa sent my grandma's letters, back in the early 1940's."

Excitement grew in Becca's voice, "This was probably a boarding house in the 1940's and she was living here. She lived on the second floor, her the return address was 30813 Watson, No. 3, upper. Oh Grif, I know this is where Granny lived as a young woman.

Grif finished his beer and said, "Yeah, maybe"

Excitedly Becca said, "This is the place, there's no doubt about it. Grif, I can feel her presence here. She lived upstairs in this very building. I found my grandma!"

Driving back towards US 1 Griff said, "The pizza was good."

Becca didn't say anything, she just stared out the side window.

Griff continued trying to make conversation with his wife, "The interior is amazing, the way visitors use markers to write something on a dollar bill then staple it on the wall. What did the server say, there's like over $80,000 covering the walls. That's a heck of a wallpaper job.

Becca regretted writing in large letters four-dollar bills, "My Grandmother lived in this building on the second floor in the 1940's!" She proudly stapled them side by side in an area she hoped no one would soon cover it with other bills.

Becca wasn't talking. In fact, she had not spoken since she read the history of the No Name Pub on the menu. "During the 1940's the second floor of the building was a brothel."

A NASTY SONA BITCH

"Man, it's raining like a mother out there," Ira said as he entered the fish shack, water dripping off his rain slicker, his tennis shoes squishing with each step. "I guess we ain't going fishing today."

The other men around the table, made up of a piece of plywood atop stacked crab pots, greeted Ira, Fat Larry with a nod, Mike with a "Hey, Ira." And Carlos said, "Ira, ya know we ain't going out fishing. Why'd ya come out in the rain. Ya shoulda stayed home with the wife."

"The old lady was talkin' bout me going up to Homestead to the Walmart with her and I didn't wanna go. So, I told her it was my day to come down and check the boat."

Mike asked, "So you would rather come out in this storm than go to Walmart?"

Wiping the rain dripping from his nose and shaking off his cap Ira said, "Oh, I like the Walmart good enough, what I don't like is spending a whole day with my wife."

Carlos and Fat Larry nodded in agreement; they knew Ira's wife.

The four men invested in a commercial fishing boat years ago. They had plans of starting a fishing business, they bought a used, really used, boat, the crab and lobster pots and all the fishing gear from Crabby Bill Whitlock's widow, when he died, fell overboard when he was out checking pots for claws. The Coast Guard found Crabby Bill's boat but not

Crabby Bill. The guys also got his fish shack, basically a weather-beaten garage down near the marina. They never started the commercial fishing business, the money they put aside to buy the commercial licenses went to repairing the boat; a rebuild of the starboard engine and the port engine was seized up, it didn't run. Hadn't in a long time, it needed it be replaced, Crabby Bill just ran the boat on one engine. The guys didn't replace it. The hull leaked and the bilge pump worked some of the time. The boat would never pass inspection to get a commercial license.

The guys just used the boat to fish for themselves, get a few crab claws and a few lobsters in season and a few out of season. Mostly what they did was sit on the boat at the marina and drink beer. Couldn't today, it was raining so they're in the shack. They like drinking beer in the shack too, it's got a refrigerator.

"The weather girl on the Miami TV station said it ain't a hurricane," Ira said.

Fat Larry asked, "That the weather girl with the big boobs or the pretty one that wears tight dresses to show off her butt when she turns sideways?"

Ira answered, "Big boobs, hell, that's the only one I watch. Mostly just to piss off the old lady."

The others showed their agreement by nodding, Mike gave a lecherous smile as his head nodded. He liked to watch both weather girls, sometimes recorded them to rewatch later.

Carlos asked, "It sure looks like a hurricane or at least a tropical storm? Look at it, it's coming down in buckets. Speaking of buckets." Carlos got up and checked the contents of the two five-gallon Home Depot buckets collecting water leaking in from the roof. Didn't need emptying yet.

A gust of wind blew the door open with rain blowing in sideways, Mike sitting close to the entrance got soaked. "Son a Bitch", he yelled and jumped up nearly tipping over the table and its collection of coffee cups.

Ira pushed the door closed. He probably didn't close it tight enough when came in. "Any coffee left?" Ira asked.

Carlos picked up the old, dented Drip O Lator coffee pot from the one burner camping stove, gave it a shake and said, "Nope."

Ira shrugged his shoulders and said, "Then I guess I'll have to have a beer," opening the old refrigerator.

Fat Larry quickly guzzled down his coffee, brown liquid dripping out the side of the cup and down his chin. Fat Larry looked in his cup and said, "Oops, cups empty, guess I'll haveta have a beer too." Carlos downed his coffee, and Ira tossed him a can. All eyes turn towards Mike.

Mike looked at his Timex, "Ya know it's only 9:48 in the morning." Mike said.

"Can't drink all day if ya don't start in the morning," Ira said popping the top of his can.

Mike agreed and accepted a beer from Ira, opened it, took a healthy swallow and asked the assembled brain trust, "Why ain't this at least a little hurricane?" He pointed out the only window of the shack that wasn't boarded up. "Lookit, it's pouring down rain and the wind is so strong it's blowing shit around."

Ira walked to the window, moved the old, weathered dock lines hanging there, used his palm to clean the glass a bit. "Cause Big Boobs say it ain't," Ira answered.

Carlos says, "To be a Category 1 hurricane its gotta be blowing at least 75 miles per hour, not in a gust, its gotta be, ah..."

"Sustained," Fat Larry helped Carlos.

Mike asked, "Then what's the speed of a Category 2, 3, 4, 5 or 6?"

"Fat Larry, check that out on your phone." Fat Larry had recently invested in a smart phone and thus far it had proved itself to be smarter than Fat Larry. He reached to his left front pants pocket saying, "Shit, musta left it at home."

"It's in your shirt pocket." Ira said pointing at the rectangular bulge on Fat Larry's chest.

Larry pulled it out of his pocket and pushed it on. He punched the four digit passcode. "Shit." Then he pushed the digits again, and a third time before he got it right.

While Fat Larry looked up the Saffin-Simpson Hurricane wind scale, the conversation turned to football. Carlos said, "The Buc's ain't looking so good this year, but the Dolphins are going to be strong."

"The Patriots are gonna take the conference this year, they always do. That new coach got "em whipped into shape, Ira said boasting about his hometown team.

Mike said shaking his head side to side, "My Bears will be contending next year, this is a rebuilding year."

"That's what you said last year," said Carlos.

Ira, spoke up, "It'll be the Lions or Packers taking the North this year."

"But, what about the Vikings? Mike asked

"96," Fat Larry says. The three men turn to Larry with puzzled looks?

"What's 96?" Mike asks, "Yer waist size?"

"No, it's his IQ," Carlos says.

Fat Larry ignores the insults. "A hurricane has to be blowing 96 miles per hour to be a Category 2."

"We're done talking about hurricanes, we're talking about football now," Ira said.

Fat Larry, blushing, is either embarrassed or his blood pressure is high, probably both. "I just found it, the hurricane wind scale. I kept hitting the wrong keys. They don't make these phones for a guy with fingers my size, ya know." Fat Larry has fingers the size of a bratwurst.

Ira asks, "What about the rest of them?"

Fat Larry looked down, the phone looks like a child's toy in his large hand, his chubby index finger swiping up. "A Cat 2 is 96 to 110 miles per hour."

He swipes up again, "Awe shit!" he exclaims. "I lost it. Just a minute." More swiping and tapping and he continues, "A cat 3 is 111 to 129. A Cat 4 is 130 to 156, and a 5 is 157 and up. There ain't no 6." Fat Larry looked up, proud of himself for being able to find the information on his phone. The other guys either don't have a cell phone or they have one that flips open they got from an advertisement in the AARP magazine.

Carlos gets up, collects the empty cans, throws them in a garbage can about to overflow with beer cans, checks the Home Depot buckets and gets a round of beer for the guys.

"Ya know, I was right here in Marathon in 1960 when Donna hit. You guys were still shoveling snow up north. Scary as shit. I thought we was going to get blown away. The wife and kid and me hiding in the bathtub, a mattress and pillows over our heads. It was a bad one. A lota damage. Lost a wall and part of the roof, and the Ford was crushed under shit. Most my neighbors houses were destroyed. A lota rain, over 13 inches."

"What was the category?" Mike asked.

"Cat 4!" Carlos said with pride having lived through a Cat 4.

Fat Larry spoke up, "130 to 156 miles per hour."

"Yeah, it was blowing 150 and sounded like a gawdamn freight train was running through the house. The wife was crying, and the kid was bawling and to be honest, I was so scared at one point I was crying too."

"Why didn't you evacuate?"

"We didn't run from em back then. Ya just hunkered down to ride it out. Last one I rode out, I tell ya. Now even if they issue a hurricane watch we're outta here. Up to my brothers in Georga."

Mike, wearing a Redbone Fishing cap with long hair curling out of the cap by his ears and down his neck asked, "When is hurricane season?"

"You live in the Keys and don't know?" Carlos asks.

"I'll look it up," Fat Larry said turning on his phone.

Carlos said, "I got this one Larry. From June 1 to November 30."

Ira asked, "Hey Carlos, I was here in 2017 for Irma, well not here, we evacuated. Have there been many other hurricanes to hit the Keys?"

"Let's see, there was Hurricane Andrew in 1992. I think it was a Cat 5. Hit up in Key Largo. Then in '98 there was Hurricane Georges, I think it was a 2 and it hit in the lower Keys. Then it was Wilma in 2005. It was only a Cat 2, not much rain but the storm surge caused a lot of damage. Irma was in 2017."

"I came down after Irma and there was damage all over." Fat Larry said. "Not a building without damage. Driving down US 1 there was piles of trash lining the highway. Waterlogged furniture, building materials, washers, dryers, stoves and refrigerators in huge piles."

Carlos said, "Hey, it was from one of those piles I pulled out our fridge." He pointed to the old Frigidaire covered with fishing stickers, tide tables a couple years old and fish shaped magnets holding yellowed pieces of paper listing who buys beer which week and who is assigned to make sure the bilge pump is working before the boat sinks at the dock.

Ira spoke up, "I was watching a show on History or Discovery about the 1935 Labor Day hurricane. That was a bad one."

Fat Larry's phone was already displaying an article about the 1935 storm. He began reading the highlights. "Estimated winds exceeding 200 miles per hour and a storm surge of 18 to 20 feet! Worst to ever hit the United States."

"I can't imagine wind over 200 miles per hour. It must have blown down everything in its path," Mike said.

"Yeah, and the storm surge washed everything into the Gulf, Carlos added. "In fact, the surge washed away part of the railroad tracks and cut new channels from the ocean to the bay. They learned that all that filling in of channels, like at the Indian Key fill, when they built the railroad wasn't good. They closed off the natural flow between the ocean and bay. So, the ocean opened it back up."

Fat Larry continued, "It destroyed just about everything from Long Key to Plantation Key."

"Where's Long Key? What mile marker?" Ira asked.

Carlos, who was a true Conch having been born and raised in the Keys, knew the answer. Plantation is about mile marker 90 and Long Key is, I think, mile marker 67. Somewhere around there."

Ira added, "So the Great Hurricane of 1935 wiped out about 23 miles of the Keys. Thats amazing."

Ira said, "The documentary said the storm killed 408 people in the Keys."

Carlos added, "Yeah, an most of 'em were World War I veterans working on the Overseas Highway in the Keys. It was some kinda work program the government had going to employ the vets. And they were down here when the storm hit and the storm surge washed a bunch of 'em into the bay.

"Didn't anyone try to warn them?" Mike asked.

"Yeah an evacuation train was sent down from the mainland but it was held up leaving and some other shit slowed it down and it arrived too late to save anyone. The storm hit while the train was still in Islamorada full of veterans. The storm surge knocked the train cars off the tracks, knocked them on their sides, all was standing was the locomotive and coal car. A lot of the tracks and railroad bridges were destroyed, there was no way in or out of the Keys. It was the worst hurricane to ever strike the United States. No other storm even comes close."

Mike stood up, took off his cap, revealing the curly hair sticking out from beneath his cap was all the hair he had on his head. He raised his beer in a toast and said, "To the World War I vets that died in the hurricane of '35. May their souls rest in peace."

The other guys followed, rising from their folding chairs. Fat Larry tried to stand up pushing down on the tabletop almost tipping it over but couldn't easily so he just raised his can with the other guys.

Carlos said in a solemn voice, "That 1935 Hurricane was a nasty sona bitch."

A BLESSING OR A CURSE

My mom had it. She said one time she thought her mom might have had it, but grandma never admitted it or acknowledged them. My brothers never displayed any signs of it, just mom and me. Mom thought of it as a blessing, a gift from God. Grandma said it was a curse bequeathed by the devil himself.

When I was just a toddler my mom knew I had it. She could tell when I was listening to them. Sometimes I talked to them. They didn't answer. I didn't know for a few years that the ghosts don't hear us, but mom and I heard them. We can't converse with them. Can't ask questions of them. I can't use them to solve mysteries. "What happened to Jimmy Hoffa." Can't ask, "Hey, ghosts, was Hoffa buried in Oakland Township, Michigan on a farm owned by a mob figure, did he, as a witness stated, run off to Brazil with a Go-go dancer, was his body in a car when it was crushed at a auto salvage yard, or burned in an incinerator, or dismembered and the parts frozen and then buried in the foundation of section 107 of the New York Giants Stadium?" Ghosts don't answer questions. It doesn't work that way. Maybe if I happen to catch Hoffa himself talking about it, I could find out.

Ghosts talk a lot amongst themselves, and we sort of eavesdrop on their conversations. It's a one-way street, we hear them, but they don't hear us. They don't know we're listening, at least they don't seem to.

They don't tell each other, "Shush, the kid is listening." They just carry on their ghostly conversations.

When I was in school the kids thought I was weird and the teachers thought I was "Special" because I would burst out laughing at something the ghosts said, or sometimes they made me cry.

I should explain that I don't always hear the dead talking. I really don't know why or when it happens. I think I might have to be in a location where they lived, died, or are buried, then I might hear them. A cemetery for me can sometimes be a noisy place. This skill or gift is not something I can turn on or off, not something I can summon up or predict. It just happens now and then. Sometimes I hear from the ghosts daily and other times they are quiet for a month or two at a time.

I've heard some really cool things from the ghosts. Like the lady who was killed in a car accident. The guy she was with was killed too. They were married, but not to each other. When I heard them apparently their spouses had died and were confronting them. Another guy was apologizing to his wife for dying while having sex. "I'm sorry honey, I left you hanging and you were almost there." I've heard confessions to crimes, arguments, dying words, and a lot of just boring conversation.

I never felt haunted by ghosts and found the programs on TV about hauntings and paranormal sightings out of whack. I've never felt threatened by the ghosts. But I'm curious about my ghostly friends. I've toured historical sites just to hear what they were saying. I learned so much, things not in the history books, like on a visit to a pre-civil war slave quarter, I heard a conversation about a war between the states was about to commence. While in Savannah, I thought I would get to hear from pirate ghosts, but they were quiet on that trip. I always heard that Key West was extremely haunted. So I thought I should make a visit and see what I can hear.

Driving down US 1 in a Mustang convertible rental car from Miami International Airport, all I heard was a lot of Jimmy Buffett and Reggae music on the radio. My girlfriend, who was not aware that I was "Special" was rockin' out in her seat playing dashboard drums and looking out the window memorized by the palm trees, turquoise water and abundance of tee shirt shops. The Florida Keys are indeed America's Caribbean.

My spirit friends were quiet. They were allowing me to just drive with the top down and the warm breeze blowing. We watched the mile marker signs count down on our way to mile marker 0 in Key West. I thought I might hear some ghost chatter as we drove south on U.S. 1since the Keys have had a long history of inhabitation on the long narrow island chain. That much human activity in such a condensed area I would think would be full of ghost talk.

There was the Seminole War, a war fought between the Native Americans living in south Florida and the settlers invading their land. The many skirmishes resulted in many deaths. The building of Henry Flagler's railroad the length of the Keys from Miami to Key West brought in many men, some of whom might have died of accidents could be talking or I thought that maybe some the hundreds of people who were washed out to sea and died during the hurricane of 1935 would be talkative. But nothing. No ghostly chatter. No voices entertaining me or sometimes frightening me. This trip might not be as ghostly exciting as I anticipated. Oh well, not all is lost. I'm going to spend a week in beautiful Key West, eat great food probably drink too much, and make love to my beautiful and adventurous girlfriend Amber.

Walking down Duval Street with Amber at my side wearing short tight shorts and a bikini top barely containing her and no ghosts in my head was refreshing. My head was swiveling back and forth looking at all the shops and bars. Amber was turning some head too.

"Oh, lets take the trolley tour," Amber said as a locomotive looking vehicle pulling open cars full of tourists passed by. Since I never denied Amber much, we made our way up Duval Street where we caught the trolley not far from Mallory Square.

As we boarded, Amber saw the sign advertising Key West ghost tours. "We need to take a ghost tour. Ryan, I know you have an interest in ghosts. I've seen you watching those paranormal shows on TV."

"I think those shows are silly," I told Amber and I doubt riding around in a trolley with a guy reading a script about ghosts will be that entertaining."

"Okay, Ryan how about taking the cemetery walk at night? I saw a brochure about a narrated walk in the cemetery. Want to do that?"

"Not really. We can walk thought the cemetery for free and read the tombstone without someone claiming to be able to talk with or see the dead."

I could see Amber getting upset with me. She was only trying to find something she thought I would be interested in. So, when she suggested we skip the tour and just walk through the cemetery and then tour the Fort East Martello Museum, I readily agreed.

The cemetery was just a short walk from Duval, but Amber insisted we stop at Irish Kevin's for an afternoon drink. Apparently, her morning Bloody Mary had worn off, or maybe she was looking for fortification to walk the cemetery, to walk among the dead.

The cemetery in Key West is a tourist attraction. Books have been written about it; brochures are available to guide the curious through the tombs. As soon as we entered off Olivia Street, I began hearing the ghosts. We passed the tombstone of Austin and Tina Griffin. They were arguing. Tina was yelling at her husband. I checked the death date on the tombstone, they died the same day in 1907. Mr. Griffin had murdered his wife then took his own life. Now he will spend eternity listening to his wife yelling at him.

There was so much chatter near the *U.S.S. Maine* Monument I could barely understand the ghosts. The American Navy Battleship was destroyed in 1898 when it exploded in Havana Harbor. Claims that the Spanish were responsible for the explosion was the cause of America declaring war on Spain.

Sailors who were injured were transported to the Key West hospital. Those that died in the hospital were buried in the Key West Cemetery.

Ryan listened to the 24 sailors that died in the Key West hospital and are buried in the Key West cemetery. They were complaining about their compatriots who were buried in the National Cemetery, and they were not.

We continued to stroll thought the cemetery. Amber read from the brochure she picked up at the gate, and Ryan listened to the ghosts.

Amber pointed out the tomb of Gloria Russel. Her epitaph read; "I'm just resting my eyes." Ryan thought to himself Gloria is not in a talkative mood today. A bit further Ryan heard a male ghost complaining, "Why won't anyone listen to me? No one believes me." Amber pointed out the tombstone of B.P. Roberts. His stone read, "I told you I was sick."

Leaving the cemetery we walked to the Fort East Martello Museum. The fort was built during the Civil War to protect the Union Army that occupied Key West from the Confederacy that surrounding them. The fort has been restored and is a museum.

We paid the entrance fee and walked around viewing the many civil war artifacts on display. There are also displays of the cigar making industry that once flourished in Key West and the history of the wreckers who raced to save cargo and crew from ships impaled on the treacherous reefs just offshore of the Keys.

Amber interrupted Ryan, listening to two ghosts talking. They were working on the construction of the fort. "Ryan, listen to this." She read from a brochure. "Robert the doll is displayed here. The doll is said to have supernatural powers. Ooooh spooky." Amber said in her best scary voice. "It's said the doll sometimes moves and changes its facial expressions. Some claim they sometimes hear Robert the doll giggling."

Ryan just gave a disbelieving smirk. Saying, "It's bullshit, just something to bring in the tourists."

"No," Amber said reading the brochure. "The doll has been studied by paranormal experts and there have been several movies and documentaries about Robert the Doll." Continuing to read Amber said, "Ryan it says here that you must show respect to Robert, introduce yourself to him, ask his permission before taking photographs then thank Robert or he'll put a curse on you."

Ryan again said, "That's bullshit."

"No, listen," Amber read further, "People who didn't show Robert the Doll the proper respect have contacted the museum reporting bad luck; divorce, loss of a job, accidents, injury and asking that the curator plead with Robert to remove the curses."

Ryan didn't believe in paranormal activities, especially in an over 100-year-old stuffed toy. "It's just a bunch of crap to sell tickets to the museum."

They found the doll encased in clear plexiglass, Robert the Doll was dressed in a sailor suit, holding a small stuffed dog, both showing the ravages of time; soiled, repaired rips. Amber exclaimed, "He's so cute! I'd take him to bed and cuddle with him all night."

As they approached the enclosure Ryan stopped cold in his tracks. He watched as the doll turned its head towards him and said, *"Hello Ryan. I've been waiting for you. Come closer, I need to talk with you. I have a job for you. There is a lady from New Jersey who insulted me, disrespected me, and made fun of me. I want her dead and I want you to kill her."*

"Ryan," Amber said, "What's wrong with you, you're pale and sweating, are you alright?

"Yes, fine let's get out of here," Ryan said as he practically ran out of the museum, thinking, "I have listened to ghosts for over twenty years, this is the first time one has talked to me. He called me by name. No ghost has ever frightened me, but Robert the Doll knew me, was waiting for me, had a job for me to do. His malicious, dreadful eyes, void of sincerity, of compassion, penetrated my soul. He was a wicked ghost, looking for a human to carry out his evil deeds."

Maybe grandma was right, what my mother calls a blessing is in fact a curse. A curse bequeathed by the devil himself, and I just met the devil."

ABOUT THE AUTHOR

Mr. Kadar is a retired professional educator, both as a classroom teacher and high school principal. He has written over 25 books ranging in subject matter from woodworking how-to-books, to novels, to books on shipwrecks of the Great Lakes, and true crimes.

Life has taken him and his wife Karen from one end of Interstate 75 in Upper Michigan at their cottage in Manistique, to the southern end of the interstate at a winter residence in the Florida Keys.

The fictional short stories gathered here have been written after decades of exploring the islands, studying the history, enjoying the natural wonders of the island chain and observing the population of the fabulous Florida Keys. Enjoy the island chain through the eyes and mind of the author.

Photograph by Karen Kadar